The First Annual Unofficial Point Pleasure Skimmer Survey and Other Stories of Cape May County, New Jersey

The First Annual Unofficial Point Pleasure Skimmer Survey and Other Stories of Cape May County, New Jersey

Ray Rebmann

iUniverse, Inc.
New York Lincoln Shanghai

The First Annual Unofficial Point Pleasure Skimmer Survey and Other Stories of Cape May County, New Jersey

iUniverse books may be ordered through booksellers or by contacting:

iUniverse
2021 Pine Lake Road, Suite 100
Lincoln, NE 68512
www.iuniverse.com
1-800-Authors (1-800-288-4677)

ISBN-13: 978-0-595-36506-7 (pbk)
ISBN-13: 978-0-595-80939-4 (ebk)
ISBN-10: 0-595-36506-X (pbk)
ISBN-10: 0-595-80939-1 (ebk)

Printed in the United States of America

"The First Annual Unofficial Point Pleasure Skimmer Survey"

I had been hacking for a tourist newspaper that summer. "Hacking" is the appropriate verb here. It recalls taxi cabs. I was a cab driver in print. My writing about the memorable experiences offered to innocent visitors to Point Pleasure led them on roundabout verbal excursions to an assortment of seasonal haunts that I, myself, did not and would never frequent; and they would avoid if they knew any better instead of placing the fate of their choices in the hands of a hack.

Point Pleasure is one of those inevitable places one finds along the New Jersey shore these days; a strip of barrier island, a sandbar. In Point Pleasure's case, the wealthy did not it buy up, fence it off, and post it off-limits to keep dune and vista to themselves and their fellow elect. Point Pleasure had maintained itself as a resort for the working classes; allowing them to briefly taste a trifling bit of surf and sand and the good life, during annual weeklong binges (two weeks if they really scrimped and saved). Point Pleasure also offered the working man illusions of what *he* can aspire to in 'anything is possible' Horatio Alger America; those illusions assuming the form of those fenced off sixteen bedroom, eight and a half bath pleasure cottages universes removed, three quarters of a mile due south in the elite section of the island named Point Pleasure Crest.

Being a hack, my literary cab never traveled to the Crest, was never called for in the Crest. For all intents and purposes, although the Crest shared the island with plebian Point Pleasure, there might as well have been a twenty foot deep moat filled with hungry tiger sharks and an electrified fence high enough to keep out King Kong, separating the two communities. Tourists, get my meaning, didn't go there; weren't wanted there; had no business there; had nothing to do there. Except gawk and wonder: how did *these* people get to be so rich.

I'm a local. Locals are a rare species who actually live on the barrier island and try to live something vaguely resembling a real life in the midst of and despite the unavoidable tourism industry. While I held the tourist in utter disdain, my livelihood depended upon his continued mindless money-squandering sprees.

That summer, I was assigned to write advertorials: puff pieces contrived to read like real news stories about local businesses. The stuff I write was really nothing more than paid ad copy. The business bought an ad in the paper. I wrote nice things about it. I did my work under a red light; allowing myself to truly immerse myself in the nature of the work I was doing. Is hacking man's oldest profession?

My writing did require creativity as my task was to depict these places in such glowing terms that visitors felt that their trips to the shore would be utterly wasted if they did not drop by to squander a sizable portion of the funds they'd scrimped, saved, or borrowed all winter to fund the trip. I used all the skills and tricks of the trade to accomplish what I did: shameless hyperbole, arcane symbolism; but mostly, out and out lying.

Did I ever feel guilty about what I did?

Let's say that I felt far worse than either of my editors, who raked in the ad money and were grateful that they didn't have to do the writing themselves. Nor did the set up bother the proprietors of the establishments in question, who gleefully scooped up tourist loot by the untaxed barrel load and, with the first hint of sunrise on Labor Day Monday; folded their tents and skeedaddled to Florida.

What did I write about? I wrote about restaurants that were textbook over and under operations: over-priced, under-quality. I called them ideal places to take the entire family...especially the kids...the more the better so long as dad brought along an armored car full of Andy Jacksons and a nurse practitioner to treat the ptomaine.

I raved about night clubs that watered the booze and jacked the prices and hired dozens of goons out of Clockwork Orange to serve as bouncers and absolutely bludgeon anyone who wasn't spending a certain number of dollars per minute and In the name of entertainment, these places offered either an overamplified band performing out of a time warp from the disco era or some one calling himself DJ Buzz who played the same 19 songs night after night on an over amplified sound system and the postage stamp dance floor was just large enough to cause a fist fight with some under age drunk who knows you're staring at some part of his girlfriend's anatomy. Such places I described as ideal and intimate spots to enjoy a delicious drink prepared by professional mixologists. Or perhaps you're the adventuresome type and want to mingle.

"Who knows, summer love might be waiting on the dance floor?" I actually wrote that. I cowered behind double-locked doors an entire weekend after that edition hit the streets.

Was I ever found mixing with the minglers? Not I. I was happily married and settled down, a pillar of the *real* Point Pleasure, the one folks doubt even exists. Being firmly anchored, I happily declared myself ineligible for admission into the joys of the typical Point Pleasure nightclub. Besides, I was usually in bed and sound asleep about the time the bartenders opened the nozzles on their hoses to prepare the evening's first cocktails.

My work at least kept pizza on the table, that delicacy having become a food staple of our summer diet.

My wife had gone off to work in the sugar mines; also known as the boardwalk fudge shop. That left me at the helm of the domestic ship. While the novelty of me in charge lasted, I managed to maintain its swervy course; using the art of overreaction as my primary navigational tool.

I was the lucky guy you read about in those magazine articles that talk about the "new world of work". I'm one of those guys who gets to work at home. It's a scam by the way. Devised by economic planners who are forever tinkering to get more productivity out of a worker than the worker would ever consider exerting on his own. Not only did I do a full-time, for pay job; I got to be a full-time house husband, too.

Household chores were no problem since these involved inanimate objects that subjected themselves to every whim and outrage I suffered upon them in the name of home economies. Meals were no problem. Point Pleasure is home to more pizza joints per square mile than any major metropolis in the United States. I could look out the front screen door and, twenty-four/seven, see the reassuring flashing lights of Vito's Pizza on the corner. Their pizza oven made tops on my list of labor saving devices I used that summer.

Handling the kids was another matter.

In the past, the kids were no problem. In the past, I wasn't around much. In the past, I'd come home from a long day at the office or at city hall covering some meeting and the kids would jump up from their homework and lovingly assault me. The wife would snarl and crack the whip at them to get back to their homework. Then she'd grab me a beer from the refrigerator and I'd kick back until dinner. In my dreams, maybe.

Anyway, school's out for summer as you may recall hearing Alice Cooper belch out, if you're old enough to remember that summer when he played at the Point Pleasure Convention Center (and why couldn't I get *that* assignment; covering the concerts with free tickets, backstage press passes, and a chance to hobnob with...Brittany Spears?). Instead, mom's off to work and I'm at home, isolated and left with only my own limited wits, to deal with the kids.

Humor worked. But after a few weeks, I learned that I had a couple of wise-cracking practical joking Robin Williams types on my hands. Their brains worked faster than mine. They were usually wittier. I had hoped to dull their sensibilities with pizza and ice cream but whenever we went out, it was like taking the show on the road. Their behavior, which *I* found gutbustingly hilarious, did not play well in Peoria, also known as the rest of the planet. Point Pleasure, after all, was a tourist town, a place where people checked whatever brains they had at the bridge leading onto the island.

The wife, putting in about 37 hours a day at her job, was too tired to notice the strain I was under and probably wouldn't have too much sympathy if she had noticed.

The kids not only had great comic instincts, their sense of pathos was finely honed as well.

"Are you going to die, daddy?" the younger one asked late one afternoon, after a particularly long slapstick skit involving play-doh and their faces, that had me sitting on the screen porch looking for a sun I could set with. I shook my head, without speaking, to give her the impression that I was seriously mulling over my options.

"Do you love me daddy?" the older one asked in my opposite ear. On cue, her eyes misted over as she gazed upon me with a look so disarming it could resolve the Middle East conflict.

"Never ask a question unless you're prepared for every possible answer." I replied pedantically, thus proving that adults can be totally boorish and minimally clever in the same sentence. Needing to retain a shred of dignity, I added, "Of course, I love you."

"We knew it!" they shouted and resumed the play-doh follies.

One or the other kid asked that question whenever they misbehaved. Sometimes, they would ask *before* misbehaving, testing the waters and providing a warning in the interest of fair play that shenanigans were in the offing. In that way, the question became part of our summer family ritual; like picking up girls in too loud nightclubs. I understood all about Point Pleasure rituals. After all, I was a hack. And a local.

"Does it matter how I behave, daddy?"

"It does. But I'll always love you. I might not be too crazy about what you're doing." Etcetera.

One particular morning, the comedy took a nasty turn. The younger girl had drawn a picture of a bird she'd seen with her summer nature class at the Wetlands Institute. The bird, she explained, had spoken to her in her dreams and asked her to draw its picture. The bird told her that the picture would make her daddy happy again. This perceptive bird went on to say that daddy was sad because he didn't like what he was doing and he missed having mommy around. The picture would make him forget being sad and he would laugh and play with his children the way he used to before he had to write nice stuff about bad restaurants. I laughed as she said all this. I wished that bird had an office with college diplomas covering the walls and a comfortable couch and some Prozac to dispense along with advice.

Most adults wouldn't have picked up on all that unless you hit them over a head with a word processor and shouted, "I hate writing this drivel about these fourth rate ptomaine parlors." While setting fire to a week's worth of copy and doing an Indian War dance.

As usual, the older sister teased the younger, a pastime that has historical antecedents reaching back to the days of Cain and Abel. In this context, the 'sacrifice' was the drawing of the bird and I was the targeted deity. The younger kid resorted to the only defenses available to her: crying and tattling.

Usually, I would put on my best Robert Young face, puff on an invisible pipe, and mediate the dispute with all the wisdom and diplomacy at my command. If the kids truly knew the limited amounts of these that I possess, World war III would have broken out in Point Pleasure.

But Robert Young's appearance had been cancelled. Instead, I yelled and hollered and said things I later realized were pretty crazy. Mom, on her way to or from work after the fifteen minute break she was granted every three days or so, gave me an odd look. The kids gave me an odd look, too. Seeing that I was serious, they started to cry.

Mom assumed command, scolded and separated the disputants, and patched things up nicely.

All that happened very quickly but we all felt a bit off center afterward. It had been one of those occurances that required distancing one's self from the group in order to attain proper perspective and analyze what happened. We were four individuals physically located in a confined area yet, mentally, we were wandering all over the place looking for clues.

Happily, such moments pass quickly because there is always a new event to push it aside and command our attention. I figured that I would be bribing the kids with ice cream and boardwalk amusement rides and the matter would be forgotten. But I wondered about possible permanent effects locked away somewhere deep inside those developing psyches. This incident just might be the first of many clues to come that dad is not the all-knowing, all-powerful wizard of Oz. They had glimpsed the man behind the curtain and found him lacking.

Truth is that disciplining kids was always an awkward chore for me. I had grown up with too much discipline and it took the Sixties for me to let loose all that outrage I felt, while being fashionable at the same time. I never struck the kids. I was always able to talk things through. Punishment, when needed, took a creative form: deprivation of privileges or goods.

Of late, though, I had become more assertive in handling discipline matters. My violence still assumed a verbal form. I'd say mean things, not meaning them; but knowing that merely saying them would hurt.

I felt like the jerk I was for doing this. But my own frustrations were coming to a head and there were the kids conveniently placed at my disposal for me to express my outrage against the unfairness of whatever happened to be treating me unfairly at any given moment.

It was *hard* to be a solid citizen, responsible parent, and productive component ofthe economy in a place where hedonism was considered a virtue and catering to vice and foolishness was the order of the day and stock in trade for all the upstanding chamber of commerce types in Point Pleasure. I often found myself looking at those gliding sailboats you always see coasting along without a care in the world at sunset and wondering how I'd feel at the helm instead of playing Pictionary with the kids.

I guess the wife escaped through her job and the zaniness of the boardwalk. On those rare occasions, when she was permitted a few hours off from her essential post as tray holder of the free fudge samples, she wanted to relax by herself. Of course, I understood. But I still resented her for asking and wondered how I'd managed to become this prisoner for life, chained to two kids.

I could have gone on like this, ranting on the inside, raving on the outside, a little while longer; but the kids rudely intruded by restarting the bird drawing controversy.

"Doesn't look like a bird." The older one announced.

"It's the bird that talked to me."

"No bird talked to you. Birds can't talk."

"This bird talked to me."

"That's not even a bird. It's a big fat blob of nothing."

"Daddy, she's picking on my bird again."

"Daddy, she's whining like a stupid baby again."

"I'm not a baby."

"Yes you are."

Coming in from the screen porch where she had been trying to rest, my wife looked at me. I just stood between the two kids, head down; shielding myself from the static whining inside my head.

"I'm going for a walk on the beach." I finally said. She sighed with relief, assuming that I had arrived at the best solution for resolving the problem; a change in venue. She turned to go back to her hammock.

The girls instantly forgot their conflict and cheered; racing for their sandals.

"Alone." I added at that second, savoring the dramatic effect.

I'd thrown them off. I never went on beach walks without them.

"Who will find the shells?" the girls asked, looking at me like the simpleton I'd become.

"Who will watch them when I go back to work?" the wife wanted to know.

"These and other mysteries will be resolved in due time by someone other than yours truly." I shrugged. And off I went; knowing that there would be hell to pay later.

So, I went beachwalking. I'd forgotten how silence sounds but recognized its tranquilizing effects as it washed over me as I strolled along the high tide line. I located a log that had been beached during a storm. I imagined exotic things on behalf of that log; that it was a ship's mast belonging to an extravagantly beyond my meager means sailboat owned by a senior partner in a Colombian drug cartel; that the boat had been bound for places I'd read about in the Travel section of the Sunday newspaper. *That* was the summer writing assignment I wanted.

I kicked the log in resentment. As it seemed to want to roll my way, I kicked it again and it rolled up to a spot among the dunes.

I sat there in the midst of gently swaying dune grass and looked out at the ocean.

No one else was walking the beach. There were no whining jet skis or ear drum popping cigarette boats annoying all mammals within 200 miles. It felt good to delude myself that I was all alone.

Looking out upon that great mass of water, I relaxed. I could actually feel the soreness in my head cool, like I'd bathed my brain in a vat of aloe oil. My eyeballs stopped feeling like a pair of ping pong balls suffering through an overextended volley at the championship match against the touring Chinese Olympic team.

The sun cooperated by establishing a mellow mood. Golden glow casually slid across the water. Suddenly, the light became a spotlight illuminating a silhouette flying along the water's edge.

The straw boater was missing. So was the exaggerated grin and leering eyes she'd learned how to draw from watching "The Best of Heckel and Jeckel" eight million times. But sure enough, there was the kid's bird, putting on an aerial show for me at dusk on the Point Pleasure beach. Just like in the picture, the bird resembled an anorexic toucan with a long thin beak that it kept poking in the water.

"Flashback." I decided, sheepishly looking about in search of some other Sixties types who might just be sharing my particular hallucination. But this show was just for me.

Suddenly, I believed in God and muttered a last good confession of every sin I'd commited since my last confession about three lifetimes ago. I was convinced that the guardian angel assigned to obliterating wicked parents was about to whack me with his flaming sword.

When there was no fiery blade shoved through my heart, I relaxed again and actually started to enjoy watching this specter flying around before me. It *was* a bird. The dammedest thing I'd ever seen; flying with its head right at the surface of the water; beak dipped in the drink as if slaking an unquenchable thirst. The bird flew up and down along the beach without ever pausing for a breather.

I watched and marveled and chuckled and forgot all my troubles. The money problems that come with buying a house that made the wife think she had to share the load by taking the boardwalk job. My work problem that caused the aggravation that led to the family problem that wasn't really a problem but had been blown out of proportion by the work problem.

It all shrank until it was a neat little package the size of a sand flea. I plucked that flea from my rapidly receding hairline and tossed to the bird as it glided by.

The bird didn't break its movement. It swerved, caught my toss in its extended lower beak, and kept right on moving. Can't hit a moving target, I admired. The bird emitted a weird call that I decided was a laugh. Then, it flew off down the beach.

I looked around and started remembering things about the beach. I remembered all the happy times I'd had there as a kid when the Point Pleasure beach was just a piker, with high tide coming up under the boardwalk at night; not the wide hot sandy desert it is today. Then, I fast forwarded to more recent memories of my own family and each time a framed scene came into focus, that bird flew past.

And suddenly, I understood certain things that I really knew already but needed a metaphysical shove to get sorted out.

I ran up the beach and down the street. Tourists headed the opposite way toward the boardwalk, parting ranks for me. I couldn't wait to get home and tell my wife and kids that life without them was meaningless. Little did I know but those inscrutable guardians of domestic bliss had already cooked something up to help me resolve the domestic crisis to everyone's satisfaction.

When I raced through the door, they greeted me cheerily, but warily. They announced that the editor of a regional nature magazine, an old college friend of my wife and godmother to my older daughter, had called. I had a new assignment.

My new assignment took me on an excursion to a stretch of beach and a jetty that was about as close to qualifying as 'deserted' as anyplace you'll find at Point Pleasure. That meant that only a few hip tourists frequented the place. These resented intrusions by anyone resembling an unhip tourist. Being a local, the difference was always lost on me.

But then, being a local meant that you never went *anywhere* in summer that might be frequented by tourists of any stripe. Locals were too busy working three jobs trying to eke out a year's income in three months to have time for such nonsense as going to beaches, hip or otherwise. For locals, beaches were the reason God created winter and Florida.

In any event, the magazine assignment was an act of mercy. Instead of dispatching me to scribble drivel about still another greasy spoon that defensively insisted that it used only the 'freshest ingredients' and did 'all its own baking on premises', I found myself writing about a migrating seabird survey.

And, in doing so, I learned about a delightful little scam.

Kirby Winston is a world-renowned ornithologist. A scion of the local Audobon Society and author of several books and numerous articles about avian behavior, Kirby came to bird watching by way of chemicals. For forty years, a particles chemist with DuPont in Delaware, Kirby had bought property in Point Pleasure Crest when it still catered to fishermen and nudists (Kirby was one of the former) and when he tired of playing with chemicals, he retired to the Jersey shore and took up bird watching.

I learned all this from my initial interview with Kirby, held near the end of a jetty at the southern tip of Point Pleasure Crest. Waves crashing threateningly at our feet; Kirby eyeing the horizon through a pair of Zeiss Laser Range Finder binoculars that would cost me the literary efforts of several summers of pride (and ptomaine) swallowing to purchase. I stood there unsteadily, trying to look natural as I jotted notes and the waves crashed sending spray over the rocks and smearing whatever I was writing.

Kirby explained that he is in charge of the "Survey". Actually, Kirby is also the originator, tax deduction underwritten donor, and sole researcher involved in the survey. Such is the level of esteem in which Kirby is held that whatever figures he turns in for his survey are unquestioningly plugged into the computer of the state agency whose function it is to maintain records of such matters as migrating seabird populations.

Aside from the pricey binoculars, Kirby's research tools are a lawn chair, a hand held calculator, a water proof notebook, and some extra strength sun screen.

"Five thousand, three hundred and twenty–two" he bellowed as he pulled his eyes from the horizon where a bird, either a pelican or a passenger pigeon I couldn't tell which, was flying low over the water's surface.

"That the count for today?" I asked.

"For the month, my boy. For the month."

"Do you break that down into species?"

"Nope. Just the birds." He proposed we take a break. That meant a short stroll to Kirby's well-appointed beachfront home and deck, complete with outdoor dry bar, well-stocked. I took a beer. Kirby took more of whatever it was that he'd been helping himself to throughout the morning.

I liked the informality of the survey and told Kirby so. He guffawed and then thrust his binoculars seaward and added another three to the count. A squadron of B-52's or albatrosses were gliding by.

"Makes it easy not having to worry what type of bird it is you're counting."

"'Migrating seabirds'. That's why I set it up that way. Let the professionals worry about how many of which." He offered me another beer. Being a freelancer, I was free to accept. If I was actually on an employer's time clock, I would have declined. *Another* advantage of working for your self.

The interview was cheerful, if not overly technical. Kirby and I discussed the socio-economic structures of Point Pleasure/Point Pleasure Crest and agreed that that old real estate maxim about 'location' truly applied on this island. Kirby went on to elaborate about 'the old Crest' and 'the new' and one knew from the disdain dripping from his voice that he sided with the old.

"These newcomers are like those birds. They fly in, take what they want without any consideration to what's here. Then they fly on. Big difference is that bird crap quickly dries up and blows away; not this tacky stuff people leave behind them."

The analogy was quotable. Kirby laughed and added another few numbers to his count. I did not happen to notice whether the latest entries were hummingbirds or pterodactyls.

"Hey Kirby," I asked, suddenly flashing upon a brilliant question as I poured brew number three and we walked a lot less steadily back toward the jetty. "How do you know if the birds you're counting aren't the same ones you counted before. You know, maybe one of those guys is on to you and keeps flying around and around the island to juice up your numbers and throw the state's computer into a tizzy."

Kirby guffawed and winked at me knowingly.

"After you finish pillorying me in your paper, stop around. Maybe you can join my survey team."

I scribbled a few more facts and figures and asked Kirby one last question about the bird I'd seen on the beach. He informed me that it was called a *skimmer.*

I pondered birds and Kirby as I typed up another puff piece and considered my personal life. My own relationship had encountered some turbulent air currents and my wings had been getting awfully ruffled lately. Humor had given way to cynicism. Maybe it was this hack job. Or maybe it was the fact of the wife, doing the eight day, twenty-five hour a day work week peddling dietetic fudge to guilt-ridden females, teevee obsessed about looking like anorexic eighteen year heroin addict fashion models. And since everyone around us was too pathetic to fairly pick on, we were on the verge of savaging one another whenever we had a few minutes to spare.

The kids were fine with us. We were fine with them. What we needed was a pleasant diversion that would allow the two of us the illusion of accomplishing something intelligent but not overly intelligent; this being Point Pleasure after all.

Kirby's survey idea was the perfect tonic.

"Take the night off, I have a surprise." I told her one night as she was between shifts.

"I hope it's not candy." She countered.

My command to take off was easier said than done. After all, this was "the season". Time to make it. No time for slacking off. Unfortunately, unlike these pseudo-humans who should really be characters in some sort of off beat "Brigadoon" musical for wannabe capitalists, we were real people who had real lives filled with meaningful activity, responsibility, and actual aspirations beyond getting to Ft. Lauderdale before October.

We didn't fit in and until this summer, had never really had to try. We felt isolated and that bothered us. What if everyone else is right?

Instead of seriously considering that prospect, I cooked up the unofficial Point Pleasure Skimmer Survey.

She had put in twenty-three consecutive days on the boardwalk and was beginning to resemble one of the so-called prizes the boardwalk bestows every Blue Moon upon some grinning halfwit who'd managed to invest about six months rent in order to win an eight foot tall pink lion that would make the ride back to Dayton or Erie or Wheeling or some other place so hopeless that getting to Point Pleasure for a week or two was actually the year's highlight and then once the drug of vacation wears off and the happy boob retrieves his prize from the car roof he is immediately puzzled. I mean, after you strut up and down the boardwalk showing off for all the other nitwits, what do you do with the dammed thing?

No, that wasn't it. She could never become so bedraggled as to resemble an eight foot pink boardwalk game prize. I guess she was more one of the delicate porcelain dolls no one ever wins, that sit on the shelf and fade from neglect. Because all the dimbulbs were too busy trying to win the pink lion and striped elephant. And I wasn't a dimbulb, so I resolved then and there not to let her fade on the shelf from neglect.

"You, my dear, are sick." I announced, as I dialed Shalimar or Beppo or whatever the Saracen, having the audacity to refer to himself as a businessman, called himself when I notified him that my wife would be in absentia.

"Never mind. She won't be there tonight." I informed him when he asked me where *absentia* was. "And she won't have a doctor's note when she does come back. You can just dock her the 37 cents or whatever princely sum it is that you thieves call a day's pay these days. Now be a nice merchant and someday maybe I'll write flattering lies about you."

I said it sweetly enough and hung up; feeling invigorated by the smooth rudeness and curtness of my telephone manner. Me, the guy who's usually on the receiving end of the modern "I'm too busy and self-important to waste my time being courteous to the likes of you" routines. Me, the guy who's too damned polite to hang up on automatically dialed calls from companies pitching stuff.

The unofficial Point Pleasure Skimmer Survey started with two pair of army surplus binoculars that her father had managed to conceal from the entire US Army during the waning days of World War II. He'd gotten those glasses over the Himalayas, through the thickest jungles of Burma, across shark-infested Pacific waters and across this country by bus. But he couldn't get them past his daughter's discerning eyes. We borrowed them for the survey and dad immediately and correctly assumed they were ours.

We were on the beach after hours. The lifeguards had shambled down from their Olympian perches overlooking the sunburned masses. The tourists heard the imaginary five o'clock whistle and the procession of lemmings returned to their hotels, motels, and camp grounds to make ready for a night on the town.

We sauntered by a sign in the dunes that read: "Whoa pardner! Help protect the native vegetation. Keep your hosses and livestock off the dunes." The sign had been conceived by Point Pleasure Public Works. It must have been an old sign from a year when the western motif was in vogue…lots of mechanical bulls and malt liquor in the bars and every restaurant in town was a steakhouse or barbecue joint. There were other signs that told people to keep off the dunes in valley girl lingo. This year's entry had to have been composed by a computer nerd as it was written in the shorthand language of the computer geek.

We chased a kid down from the dunes, where she was playing directly in front of the keep off the dunes sign. Her mother gave us a dirty look but truth, justice, and the American system were on our side.

Public Works had created dunes at every street block by scraping sand into huge mounds in hopes that the next tropical storm wouldn't simply wash them away.

Of course, indifferent nature never cooperated but it kept a couple dozen locals gainfully employed, each with his very own bulldozer.

Always reminded me of Hemingway when I saw them. You know. The line about adults being little more than big kids playing with fancier toys. Those dozers making dunes made about as much sense as two kids with pails and shovels paddling about a sand castle they built at water's edge. Watch the wave come up and wash it away. Watch the kids run crying to mommy and daddy. Only taxpaying chambers of commerce, demanding beach maintenance, cry a helluva lot louder.

We found a nicely isolated niche in the arms of one of the dunes where we could sit facing the ocean and keep out of the wind. The neon bustle of the Point Pleasure boardwalk was obliterated from view. This was probably the only spot on the beach where such isolation could take place. A perfect place to watch for skimmers. I brought along a twelve pack of Rolling Rock to help us with our math. We no sooner spread our blanket and fetched out the binoculars when a police patrol jeep pulled up, looking very much like an apparition out of the Twilight Zone.

"Whatcha doin?" a surly Rod Serling asked, eyeing us like we were creatures from another dimension.

I was ready for this. Point Pleasure cops are famous for being as far away from potential crime scenes and other distasteful hotbeds of human hyperthyroid activity as the laws of physical science and the geography of barrier islands will allow. I fully expected to see them on the beach, after hours, when there was a small likelihood of anyone being about; all the tourists having pavlovially scooted off to the sundry places I'd been hacking about all summer.

"Skimmer survey." I announced self-importantly, flashing my press card. "I'm doing an in depth story on migrating seabirds, skimmers, in particular. Contact Kirby Winston. He'll fill you in on the details."

I haven't done much learning in this life and I learned even less in college. But one thing I was born knowing is that cops don't give two hoots about birds. Now, if I told them I was waiting to interview the fourth string punter for the Philadelphia Eagles, they would have been thrilled to death. They also would have hung around. However, the prospect of watching us watch birds removed us as objects of curiosity. Contempt, certainly; but not curiosity. And since it's apparently written in the Book of Cops that bird-watchers are law abiding, albeit goofy, they left us alone.

Rynchops nigra nigra is slender, white and black. He has a scissors-like bill, bright red and tipped with black. The lower mandible juts out about one-third farther than the upper. The skimmer flies low over the water. The lower mandible cuts through the water like a knife. Like a shovel is more like it. They eat crustaceans.

The skimmer has long wings. From the tip of the tail to the tip of the beak, the typical skimmer is 18-20 inches long.

So much for the birdwatcher book, Kirby Winston's in this case.

You don't hear much about skimmers because they tend to be the aloof type even though their nesting areas are within close approximation to the summer homes and pleasure palaces of millions of humans. I especially admired the way they waited for the humans to leave the beach before taking over, very inconspicuously.

Skimmers, like teenagers, like to breed on coastal beaches. Other favorite trysting spots include sandbars, shell banks, and gravel rooftops.

We returned to our home that first night of the survey and it was the total quiet that reminded me that the kids were spending the night with their grandparents. This was the *big night out* for me and the wife.

In the dark outside, I stripped naked. Hanging up the wet beach towels and swim suits, I immediately began imagining myself as some sort of awkward aborigine, furtively finding my way in the dark and feeling vulnerable in my nakedness. Now I know why lawyers always look silly when they're not in their three piece suits.

The clouds above assumed fantastic dusk shapes as the setting sun played last minute light games with them bending and twisting their silhouettes into all sorts of delightfully weird shapes resembling every animal that ever lived in the twilight realm of imagination. I lost myself in those clouds and the growing darkness and my own cool nakedness; holding a wet beach towel bearing the likeness and logo of some Disney character. Then, my wife pulled an Edison on me and switched on the outside light. She was startled and then reduced to giggles by my animal scream of rage, fear, and pain. Spotting me naked, she gave a shrill whistle and called out to the neighbors before returning to the house with a sinister laugh.

She then flicked off the light, stripped herself naked and joined me in the middle of what we brazenly called our garden, as if such a thing can possibly exist in the compressed space professional planners and developers define as building plots in places like Point Pleasure.

Our relationship had been on the rocks and we were so busy doing stuff that we didn't even have time to realize that. Fortunately, with the survey, we were able to relocate from those rocks every afternoon to the softer, more form accommodating sand dunes. With our sole "function" being to watch and count skimmers, and no need to be overzealous on either count, we found ourselves with plenty of time to talk and even things to talk about. That led us to more important things to talk about and we discussed and argued and debated and shared secrets like teenage lovers and so resolved numerous conflicts both local and global. Greenpeace would have been proud of us.

We journeyed a long way together in a short period of time since embarking upon the survey. Our first night's discussion had centered on detailing things we didn't like about one another. It was an awkward and sometimes painful exercise in honesty; the kind of honesty that most couples, including us up until then, went to great lengths to avoid. It started as a game of 'what I don't like about you…'

"I don't like the way you waste water."

"I don't like the way you throw towels all over the bathroom."

"You snore and toss and turn."

"You do the dishes all wrong."

"You can't cook."

"You can't fix anything around the house."

"You're always late for things that matter to me but you're a pain about being on time for things that matter to you."

"You always complain but never follow through."

"You don't discipline the kids enough."

"You can't cook."

"You're getting fat enough."

It was a very productive exchange. Everything we said was true and everything we didn't say but could have was also true and we knew each other well enough to understand the significance of what we *didn't* say. We each resolved to work on our shortcomings; toasting our newfound understanding with a cold Rolling Rock.

"*You* were supposed to get ice." I teased.

She held up a white towel in surrender as seventy-nine skimmers slipped by, uncounted.

In addition to skimmers, we included as part of the count for the unofficial Point Pleasure skimmer survey: someone's escaped pet macaw that took a liking to us and frequently joined us on the blanket; a laughing gull with a pronounced lisp; two brown pelicans that, seeing the far more efficient fishing technique employed by the skimmer, attempted to imitate it, often with hilarious results; and a harrier that menacingly soared over us frequently as we had frightened off the local rodent population.

Each night, we'd sit back and drink a beer and wait for the first night's skimmers. The brash lights from the hotels and boardwalk faded into honky tonk insignificance when shown in contrast to the inky depths of approaching night over the silent ocean.

Wading waist deep into the sea, its warm night waters flow gently around us as a full moon rises directly ahead; extending long golden fingers glittering from the horizon and passing all around us as we swam out to the sand bar and tread water.

Last glow of the sun from behind as the sky colors faded to velvet and we contemplated Jupiter rising. Then we spotted skimmers.

They glided effortlessly in groups of four and five, hunting their evening meal; their dark silhouettes unmistakable as they passed between us and the rest of the world. We looked at one another without speaking. Speech would ruin it.

I knew then that I would be writing this now and knew then that my words would be woefully inadequate to express the feelings of that moment. Which is what the survey is about.

We talked together as we rode waves to shore. We said in shorthand that we would rather be skimmers than acknowledge fealty to the 21st century. Not voiced was our contempt for the "time saving gadget"; that makes human experience a form of obsolescence.

Just then, the Point Pleasure beach tram chugged across the beach.

The Point Pleasure beach tram has its own life-support system with the operator sealed into an air-conditioned sound proof compartment. He reads a script prepared by the Point Pleasure Public Relations officer, extolling the wonders of nature even while being utterly cut off from the environment his machine trampled, on its hourly sight-seeing tours through that environment. And right behind the tram, a similarly equipped vehicle scooted along and, with a tenacious steel claw, took up the contents of nearby trash cans and emptied them into its open belly. The friendly operator waved. He wore headphones and listened to tapes of ocean sounds while on the other side of his thick Plexiglas cocoon sand, water, and wind, the cackle of gulls, the smells of salt and algae washed ashore by the latest tide now waiting to be scooped up in the morning by still another machine designed to preserve a sterile, pristine beach that tourists go gaga over.

Just over the vehicle, yet a universe removed, a least tern battled a gull for fragments of mullet.

We ignored the machine the way we tell our children to ignore bad dreams and go back to sleep, planting good thoughts for them to use in their dreams.

We watched the birds scuffle and added the tern and gull to our count for the skimmer survey.

On many nights, we violated the law and enjoyed an after-hours swim as watery darkness swallowed us up, caressing us. I'd sit holding my breath on the ocean floor, eyes open, and watch waves roll by. They resemble film footage of cumulus clouds speeded up a hundred times.

Then, after we felt all our tension seep out of our pores and wash out to sea, we floated where dark sky meets dark water and allowed us the illusion of weightlessness, and we talked about our children.

"I watched Amanda the other day at her friend's birthday party…she's really shy, isn't she?"

"She's not like the other kids. Hates soccer for one thing. And since we don't watch television, she doesn't understand what they're talking about half the time."

"She's at the social age. She needs to feel like part of the crowd."

"She's in scouts."

"That *was* scouts. She doesn't fit in…"

"Because *we* don't fit in."

"Do you *want* to fit in?"

The pause was eloquent. It didn't matter which of us was saying which line in this dialog. The kid was being something of a pain in the ass at home and we're not sure why; hence, the need for discussion.

We considered showing more empathy and understanding. The mere fact that we're using such words speaks volumes for the mellowing effects of the illegal swim, of the entire unofficial skimmer survey.

"You know what my father says?" she interjected.

"Who, old woodshed Charlie? The great child psychologist. Yeah, I can imagine how tactfully he'd handle something like this. A whole generation that lived by the cat o' nine tails and what did it get them. Us and the Sixties."

"You didn't turn out so bad."

Ours was a problem shared, in varying degrees, by all well-intentioned parents in the modern world. How far do you go to protect your kids from that modern world?

There is some wisdom to the theory of letting kids "get out there" and experience things for themselves. Sure, they'll get burned but they'll also learn.

But this isn't the world of Mark Twain. A kid can't just build himself a raft and go sailing down the great Mississippi of Life. Without going into our own laundry list of grievances against the way the modern world deals with children, we agreed that there had to be control.

We were Sixties kids, though. 'Control' is a dirty word. We'd have had our mouths washed out with organic soap back in our hippie commune days for even whispering so foul an utterance.

Truth is, we were running a pleasant little concentration camp for minors.

A skimmer glided past, mullet tail dangling from its mouth. We crawled up into the dune, knowing that the bird would circle behind us and bring the fish to its nest where its young ones hungrily waited. Nothing like a bit of pre-chewed regurgitated sushi for dinner to make a kid eager to find its wings and be off on its own, I always say, as the stuff passed from beak to beak.

I washed the scene down with a healthy gulp of beer and jotted some stuff in my notebook.

"Let's try that on the kids." I teased. "It'll probably go down easier than that gruel of yours."

She pinched me and then hushed me before I could retaliate.

"You have to go with them everywhere, even school, because you can never be sure." She said in a serious tone. "A kid's birthday party might turn out to be a drug dealer's house. A scout leader could be a pedophile. You can't assume anything anymore. Teachers, ministers, the kindly old gentleman who lives in the house on the corner."

"I know." We didn't even let our kids ride their bikes around the block without one of us tagging along. "It's sick. But if you do your job right, protect them and teach them without scaring the hell out of them, they'll come out okay."

"But I keep worrying about them missing out on things; like the chance to be on their own; the chance to fail and come back."

"They'll have plenty of that. Our job's to get them to the point where they're ready to try. They're too young for that now. Too many kids start too early and it warps them. Got all these eight year old adults running around. Let 'em be kids."

The skimmer was teaching its young ones how to fly. I watched through the glasses as my wife made some notes for Kirby Winston. We dutifully noted that there were more and more skimmers in that particular section of beach each time we reported for survey duty.

By then, the beer was gone and it was night. We couldn't see a skimmer if a tribe of them pitched tents and camped on our shoulders.

Skimmers tend to return year after year to the same nesting areas unless the colony has been attacked, in the past, by predators. That possibility is increased by the fact that skimmer "nests" tend to be unprotected scraped areas in the sand. A more elaborate nest will include shells as a camouflage.

What the crew members of the unofficial Point Pleasure Skimmer Survey hadn't counted on was that the birds would choose a stretch of beach directly behind our spot for their nesting site. That started the Point Pleasure Skimmer Survey dune fencing project. The excitement coming through from the other end of the phone when Kirby Winston referred us to the state Fish and Game Department convinced us that we had saved the planet. We were asked to guard the nesting area with our lives until one of Trenton's 'top men' could reach the scene. The Point Pleasure Skimmer Survey had been made 'official'.

The guy down from Trenton was amazed at how many skimmers had chosen a beach in such a heavily populated area, albeit one that was less frequented because of its width; beachgoers hated to walk an extra city block to cross it to the water.

"What does it all mean?" I asked, tongue in cheek, not expecting an attempt to answer such an empty-headed, open-ended question.

"It means the skimmers are behaving abnormally. Perhaps their nesting practices are changing in response to habitat loss and the lack of good nesting sites in coastal areas."

"Perhaps they're making a statement about humans ruining the beach."

I guffawed. One well-aimed bulldozer would quickly put an end to the skimmers' so called "statement". But I had to admit that my wife and I loved the romantic lunacy of the idea. I decided to rework my puff piece on Kirby Winston to so reflect the idea.

My editors fell for it. Not that they understood or particularly cared about "the technical bird stuff". But the chance to tweak the collective noses of the Jersey shore and the grubby way it conducts its tourism industry…*that* they understood completely.

I was told to stay with the guy from Trenton and write about what happened.

"Went hunting for the first time this year." He informed us in an accent that came straight from a Connecticut suburb. "There's nothing like killing and preparing your own meat. It was a viscerally stimulating experience."

As the DEP expert regaled us with his "Mark Trail" tales, my wife and I rolled our eyes and suppressed giggles, wishing they'd sent Jane Hathaway instead of Grizzly Adams. But he was eager to do the hard work; namely, talking to public works and police; who wanted to know what we were doing and by whose authority. For them, he waved a badge and proclaimed that he was from 'the state'. Then he put on his public relations hat and tried educational outreach which pissed off tourists who couldn't understand 'why all the fuss over some birds'. Finally, we were encountered by a truly furious mayor.

While my wife, the kids, and I pounded in the last of about three hundred fence posts around a very wide nesting area, the expert debated the mayor. Curiously, the mayor backpedaled when I poked my head into the fray and informed him that I worked for a great metropolitan newspaper and would be doing a front page feature story on how the great resort town of Point Pleasure welcomed an endangered species that had adopted a small part of its beach. He hopped, skipped, and jumped away from me like a toothless, clawless piping plover trying to sidestep a hungry predator and dance away to safety.

The mayor hemmed and hawed and finally agreed with the arrangement as long as it did not interfere with the tourists and then he hastened away but not before inviting me to his office for a few quotes and lots of spin.

It was then, for the first time, that I was truly impressed by the power of the press.

"The great equalizer." I mused as the expert scratched his head and pondered his latest 'viscerally stimulating experience'.

That night, we brought the kids to the beach to help us with the survey. What had started out as 'mommy and daddy night out' became a family outing based upon the very successes of our earlier survey evenings. We had purged ourselves and become certain of who we were and where we wanted to be. The survey had helped us remember that we were lovers and friends who could work together through any situation no matter how serious or outlandish. We were also parents. And we knew that our kids now needed to join us in our adventure.

MY story played out as one might expect circus-caliber scenarios to unfold. It became another one of those spotted owl versus greedy axe-wielding capitalists by the time the wire services picked it up. Conservative radio commentators lambasted the knee-jerk ecoterrorists who dared to allow such a useless bird to encroach upon priceless real estate and impeded the always forward march of progress to puritan heaven as conceived by every right thinking American. Television people, preening their hair and wearing inappropriate beach footwear descended upon Point Pleasure, in search of sound bytes and instead, received mosquito bites. Most retreated to their helicopters and hovered over the nesting area; thus impeding any of the activity they hoped to film. The skimmer was getting its fifteen minutes and then some.

In all of this, Point Pleasure took a beating. The resemblance of one particular skimmer, a darling with camera people, to the toucan whose image adorned a very popular kid's cereal box, didn't help any. The city fathers wrung their hands at secret emergency meetings. One overzealous public works employee volunteered to go to the beach one night and shoot the birds. Another suggested that the area be bulldozed but done in such a way as to make it appear to be an act of God. Remembering the last time, local officials attempted to interfere with nature by tossing chlorine tablets into the ocean to "fix" the weekly fecal coliform tests taken by the Health Department, the mayor quickly squashed that idea.

The city fathers were ham-handed men; of the "can-do" spirit who believed that all problems had solutions; that things that didn't work to their satisfaction could be fixed or, if not, discarded and disposed of and no obstacle should be left standing in the path of the hard-working businessman exercising his God-given right to make a profit.

Now, if only someone would straighten out these damn birds.

Having no idea how birds speak or think, having lost all contact with the natural world in their midst, a world which still insists upon intruding itself into their neat ledger realities the city fathers had no idea where to turn.

Giggling pied pipers, my wife and I stepped forward.

We entered the Chamber of Commerce building, heathens in the house of the holy. We had no business being there. But *we* understood the birds or at least, *they* were so out of touch with anything that didn't have a dollar sign that they were easy to convince that we understood the birds.

Call it my innate cynicism or symptoms of having been on the island too long, the things I said to them were things they needed to hear.

"Tourists are dumb. They'll fall for anything if you present it to them the right way. You, Mr. Mayor, weren't you partners in a bungee jump a few summers back before that lady busted her back and sued you and the state came in and closed you down. Didn't you see those people lined up for three blocks waiting for the chance to fork over $60 so they could jump off the top of a crane with nothing to keep them from splattering all over the boardwalk except a giant rubber band."

"And you, Hal Singley, didn't you use to go up the Poconos every April and bring back truckloads of rocks and sell them as pets at $7 apiece. And you Mr. City Attorney, didn't you pay your way through law school running coat hangers up all the leashes you got from the city after the dog catcher carted the strays to the pound, and sell them for $12.99 each as 'invisible dogs'?"

"You guys have become so sanctimonious with this family resort quality vacation drivel that you've forgotten that Point Pleasure's really just a two bit carney town and you guys are a bunch of hucksters. Why turn away from that now? It's as American as corporate welfare and gas-guzzling SUV's."

"Make the most of those birds. It's why God put 'em there."

It was the speech of a lifetime. I could hardly contain my laughter. But they swallowed it all; hook, line and sinker. Even the part where I called them two bit hucksters. They knew. They knew. And I know. Guys like me have been paid to make bozos like them look good and they'd been believing their own press releases.

On the spot, I was hired to be Point Pleasure's official public information officer at a salary that made me blush redder than that light I kept burning over my word processor to remind me what the stuff I wrote *really* was.

Survivors adapt. Nowhere is that maxim truer than in the murky business of the tourism industry. It came as no surprise that, once the media began waxing poetic about skimmers and public sentiment embraced the critters, local business was swept up in skimmer mania.

There were skimmer t-shirts, of course. With every third store on the three mile long Point Pleasure boardwalk selling overpriced t-shirts, the competition was fierce. Soon, the skimmer was outselling perennial favorite: "I'm With Stupid" (with the arrow pointing at whomever happened to be walking beside the wearer). In addition to the "nature" look shirt featuring skimmers flying as only skimmers fly; there was the comedy shirt showing the skimmer beak submerged in a mug of beer as it flew into a bulkhead. Or there was the skimmer riding the roller coaster or slurping name brand ice cream; gobbling pizza; or sloshing down soft drinks. All skimmer beaks bearing the Point Pleasure logo.

The shirts were just the start. Boardwalk games of chance offered stuffed animal skimmers as prizes; replacing those eight foot pink lions, purple dinosaurs, and striped giraffes on the roofs of vehicles heading back to Dayton, Erie, or Wheeling.

The beach tram added a visit to the nesting area, including special moonlight tours, all of which featured a real live naturalist from the nearby community college, offering lite avian repartee to trysting trammers.

Beachfront motels lucky enough to have unobstructed views of the nesting areas cashed in and offered customers complimentary binoculars so guests could lounge at the pool and enjoy the "madcap antics of Point Pleasure's native sons and daughters".

Local taverns offered special drinks using rums and liquors and fruit mixers that, when blended just so, gave the drink the coloration of the celebrated bird. Complimentary straws in the shape of skimmer beaks came free with each drink. Restaurants offered skimmer salads and "skimmer hours" during which meal prices were reduced and stuffed toys were given to every kiddie under age of twelve who ordered from the kiddie menu.

The Point Pleasure Chamber of Commerce proudly announced the first annual Skimmer Hatching fair and Crafts Show. It featured a special kids' skimmer coloring contest and a name the first born skimmer contest. There was a skimmer costume and mating dance contest for adults and more than a hundred street vendors selling anything that wasn't nailed down.

It was a heady time. I had a hand in conceiving each and every one of these gimmicks, even down to writing the mayor's speech to the state's newspaper editors convention which awarded Point Pleasure a prize for innovative marketing. It was all me. I was responsible and I felt absolutely lousy about it.

I went to visit Kirby Winston one day and found him, drink in each hand (one for me) bellowing on the jetty as he counted flying v-formations of southbound Canadian geese.

"Gotta goose the numbers a little." He joked.

He then turned and thumbed his nose in a ceremonial gesture at his neighbor's house and invited me to share his scorn.

A new palace had been built next to Winston's much more modest beachfront abode. It was a three story birthday cake made out of solid marble. It contained nineteen bedrooms, nine bathrooms, twelve decks, ninety-seven windows, several Jacuzzis and hot tubs, a heated outdoor swimming pool, and a helicopter landing pad on the roof.

"Brought all that marble over from Italy." Kirby said. "Look at it. Used to be, the fishermen would come here and build a one room shack out of driftwood or whatever else washed up on the beach. They'd live in it through the season and leave and let nature do what it would. Now they bring marble from Italy and build these Xanadus and the owner isn't there more than a day or two a year."

"See that heliport. He'll land there and then, I guess, spend twelve minutes in each of his bathrooms and then leave. Probably doesn't even know where he is. If you went in there and told him that was the Indian ocean out there he'd believe you because he hasn't a clue. Just lots of money."

Kirby was mad. Mad about the arrogance and the waste. Mad that his tax money was being used to subsidize his neighbor's flood insurance and the guy probably wrote the whole place off anyway.

"A thousand years from now, archaeologists are going to go diving there and sixty feet down at the bottom of the ocean they'll find this marble monstrosity and wonder who would have been stupid enough to build such a thing so close to the ocean."

Kirby laughed and congratulated me on the success of my campaign and predicted that if I 'kept my nose to the grindstone, I'd end up in a marble palace of my own'.

"As for me, I'm selling this place and moving to central America. More types of birds there. Probably write a few more books and do a tropical songbird survey in some jungle or other." He guffawed and emptied his glass.

I announced my resignation from my public sinecure and burned the ski mask I'd worn every time I cashed my pay check at the bank.

That night, I turned off the word processor and the answering machine and the e-mail. The wife and I took our kids, our kayaks, and a picnic basket to the beach. We ate and played and swam and paddled the kayaks out beyond the breakers. While we sat floating in that calm water, we heard the noise from Point Pleasure in the distance. Dolphins circled us and began to play in the waves. The kids squealed in delight and ran their fingers along the dolphins smooth bodies as they glided that close among us. We played together in the water and on the beach late into the night. It had been a long time since we'd felt so close with one another.

Just as night fell, we saw skimmers flying along the water's edge. Hundreds of them rising over the dune from their nesting area. More and more of them poured onto the beach and skimmed along the surface of the water. They flew back and forth in front of us several times. Then, rising up into the sky, they formed a giant cloud and sped away to the southwest, vanishing behind a rising full moon.

Skimmers never returned to nest on that beach. The unofficial Point Pleasure Skimmer Survey was quickly forgotten. The Chamber of Commerce authorized a new marketing scheme that reflected Point Pleasure's newest fascination, with the Roaring Twenties as the focal point of the next summer's promotional campaign. Even the professional nature lovers were too busy applying for grants and picking up bureaucratic kudos for their efforts in bringing attention to the plight of the skimmer to bother with the actual work of tracking the birds after they'd moved on.

In short, the skimmers were soon forgotten by everyone but me.
And my wife.
And my kids.

"Fading Glimmerings of a Dying Breed"

Before Point Pleasure became an overdeveloped tourist trap along the Jersey shore, it was a small settlement of ramshackle stick shacks that no self-respecting fairy tale wolf would consider blowing down. The mere whisper of the word "northeaster", the tiniest rumor of a hurricane brewing in the faraway Gulf of Mexico, was enough to tumble down all four dozen of these seasonal shanties erected on the sand bar.

That was seasonal housing in the truest sense. Not even a real estate sales wiz, enshrined in his profession's Million Dollar Club, could pass off these structures as anything more than temporary: one summer lease, take the 6% and run for cover before the big blow.

There was a method to the madness of those earliest visitors to New Jersey's barrier islands. They did not squander precious time constructing twenty-three room (five bathroom) summer mcmansions, complete with jacuzzi, dry bar and in ground swimming pool three hundred feet away from the second largest free swimming pool in the Solar System.

The first white visitors to the barrier islands were Viking fishermen who had no intention of living on such inhospitable places. These were sand bars for Christ's sake. No doubt, these were roughhewn men, illiterate and coarse in their language. But they were not stupid.

They threw up tiny stick lean-tos to shield themselves from the elements while they tarried in the area and fished. Once the fish were caught and dried and packed away, the fishermen left the shacks to their own devices until they returned the following year and rebuilt them from whatever scraps happened to have washed up.

The waters around what would become Point Pleasure were teeming with fish of all sizes, shapes, and dispositions a mere 300 years ago. Fishermen came and went as they pleased. They needed no permits to fish. There were no government agencies monitoring the size of their catch to determine if they were legal "keepers". There were no environmentalists speaking out on behalf of the fish. There were no deeds, easements, leases, or licenses. There were men and fish and the elements that bound them together in their life and death struggle.

They had come for the biggest prize the planet offered, land or sea: whales! The first settlement on the island was called Whale Point. The winds and sands of time have wiped the island clean of that community that never really was. By the time the fishermen left, moving north to more promising waters off New England or inland to take up less precarious pastimes, the whales were gone, too.

The barrier island was left to its own devices which included the generous application of wind and water and sand, to reshape itself and await the next coming of humans who would apply themselves to using it to satisfy whatever whims happened to motivate them.

An old man, wearing a windbreaker, huddled in his collar as the wind gleefully sculpted billions of grains of sand off the berm of the federal government's most recent mulitimillion dollar sand dune replenishment project at the affluent north end of Point Pleasure. The wind carried that sand down to the honky tonk low rent district at the south end of the island where the beach was already wide enough to build another town between the bulkheads and the high tide line.

The locals snickered about that; suggesting that the rich folks, newcomers passing through on their way to more fashionable holdings up at the point, could have as much sand for their beach as they were willing to buy by the truckload.

This old man in the windbreaker was oblivious to all that. Just as he was oblivious to the howling cry of the wind and roar of the nearby sea. He concentrated instead on electronic clicks and beeps coming through a set of earphones that disconnected him from the sounds around him and hooked him up to the alien music of the gadget world.

Beamish was a modern day, small scale treasure hunter; seeking loose change and bits of jewelry that careless tourists leave behind after summer visits to the Point Pleasure beach. He'd never found more than a dollar or two, once a high school ring. Being a retiree, treasure hunting gave him something to do and kept him out of his wife's hair so she could devote herself to her day's chores, television talk and soap. It also got him out of doors in the fresh air where he could interact with the elements.

Beamish hated the elements. Hated the sand and the salt spray. Hated the screeching and bad manners of the gulls. Hated the sticky feel of salt water. Hated the smell of millions of once living things that accumulated to decay at the rack line before the city's public works crew scraped them up with bulldozers and carted them off to who cared where. Beamish gloated over that, over the way that man had subjugated nature, even here at the edge where the supposedly big bad wild ocean raged only to be tamed by the hand of man's engineering and his mightier machines.

Beamish was proud of his own long and dedicated role in keeping those machines constantly well-oiled, running and improving.

Beamish wondered why he had come to this place to die. Oops, *retire*! That nice euphemism for dying. All of them: the doctors, the insurance company, the employer to whom he'd shown unfailing loyalty for almost forty years labor in a machine shop; his kids, now grown and having no further use for him, eager to discard him...even the wife. Ready to take his pension check and Social Security check and run off to Florida and play Bingo for the rest of her life.

This beach was good for one thing, he thought ruefully. It allows a man time and space and enough fresh air to clear his head and see things as they really are. Too much air, too much time, he thought. Too much clarity. His thoughts alternately annoyed him with their meanness or bored him with their petty ordinariness.

Beamish was not comfortable with himself in these raw elements. He needed machinery; something to tinker with. He thrilled to the sound of the metallic ticks and clicks and buzzes of this electronic detector he'd rigged up in his shop. It featured a different sound for each type of metal he figured on encountering. This beat walking a dog, he mused.

For one thing, the machine didn't want to drag him on a merry chase through the dunes after rabbits. It didn't splash water all over his new shoes as it played in the waves.

It didn't retrieve smelly dead things for him to admire before racing off to retrieve more smelly dead things. The machine stayed right with him and spoke only when it had something worth saying.

Beamish derived great satisfaction from the fact that he had designed and built this metal detector himself; especially the computer-like device that could actually discriminate between different metals hiding beneath the shifting sands of this god-forsaken beach. Special clicks announced silver. A gentle buzz revealed those peculiar alloys that went into the making of modern coins. An annoying beep warned him of aluminum or some other "junk" deemed disposable these days. Beamish recalled the war years and the collection drives for various materials and shook his head at the extravagant waste of today's society, all the while promoting it in the name of its concept of "resource scarcity".

"Only thing scarce nowadays are young people with ingenuity to think through a problem and willingness to put in an honest day's work." He muttered as he swept his magic wand over the flowing sand, hoping to turn up a bit of treasure.

Gold was the one metal he'd neglected to program his detector to find. He hadn't figured on finding gold on this beach. After all, this was Point Pleasure. Maybe up at the north end. The beach was privately owned there, and fenced off in sections like so many pastures for sunburned rich cattle. But down at this end where the shoobies come to the beach carrying their belongings wrapped in a beach towel to enjoy a quick dip before heading back to the buses that would shuttle them back to their cities.

On this beach, the most Beamish figured to find was a few coins, a boardwalk skeeball token, maybe some cheap jewelry.

He was surprised the morning the machine went berserk. The tide was an exceptionally low and Beamish had wandered down to the very edge where he had to dodge the surf to keep his shoes from getting wet. No telling what's been laying here over the years, he thought. When the machine made noises indicating something its programming didn't recognize, Beamish became excited.

Whatever it is is big, he thought. Beamish applied the spade he carried to dig up the machine's finds. Water handicapped his efforts but he managed to get a pretty good hole going. He was surprised at how deep he was digging. Fortunately, the tide was still outgoing, so the ocean bothered him less and less, as it peeled back to reveal its many secrets.

Finally, he struck something hard, bigger than a baseball.

It felt like a rock. It was heavy but not quite as heavy as a rock this size might be expected to be. It was about the size of his gnarled fist.

"Probably a rust-crusted part from a boat." Beamish grunted, eager to get at it.

He scraped away sand until he reached the object itself. Feeling its contours, he studied the object through a magnifying glass, frowning. He had no idea what he held in his hands and not knowing gnawed at him.

As he lifted the object to the sunlight, he caught a glint of something shiny. It was still mostly crusted with sand but there was a hint of a once bright metal that could not be tarnished even by the scouring sands of time

"A poet now." He smirked, that image of time's sand running through his mind.

...Sometime between the Viking fishermen and the arrival of tourists, pirates frequented the waters off New Jersey. Many were ragtag privateers but there was an outstanding achiever in the bunch: William Kidd.

There is a story about a solitary sperm whale that used to shadow the ship of the notorious pirate, as he raided up and down the east coast, slipping in and out of concealment among the many inlets and back bays of the coast of New Jersey. No one knew these waters like the crew aboard that ship. They ventured into places where no white man had ever gone before.

Perhaps there was some primordial funk permeating that ship that attracted the great leviathan. Perhaps it was the whale's own solitariness that drew him to seek the companionship of other mammals. Perhaps it was that Kidd's men, single minded in their pursuit of treasure, did not try to kill the whale; instead adopting it as a mascot; the whale assuming their behavior to be evidence of some higher (cetacean) level of intelligence.

It is said that the Indians, who once dwelled in harmony with this region, used to travel to the shore each year to sing with the whales. Perhaps this monster genetically recalled those blissful times and believed the pirates were seeking a similar communion...

By the time Beamish reached home, his imagination was racing, an unfamiliar experience for that particular mental faculty. He was full of what he knew were impractical fantasies that provided such a shock to his thoroughly pedestrian mind that he had to remind himself to stop the car's motor and remove the keys from the ignition before he sprinted out to his garage workshop.

The wife heard him panting heavily from the excitement and was about to dial 911 for the rescue squad when he called her out to the garage. She *really* worried then. Beamish had never invited her to visit the inner sanctum of his workshop in all their forty-six years of wedded bliss.

She threw on a shawl and raced out, expecting to find her husband slumped over in purple-faced apoplexy. Instead, Beamish was hunched over the work bench scratching away with hammer and chisel at a sand-covered rock. She frowned and turned to go back to her ironing when he called her to take a look.

"It's a whale's tooth." She told him matter of factly as she examined his find.

"What? How do you know that?" He asked peevishly.

"I was born and raised here, wasn't I? My daddy and his daddy were fishermen, weren't they? They was always bringin' home strange stuff they dragged up off the bottom of the ocean. *You* think I never saw anything. It's a whale tooth. My brother used to have a whole collection of 'em."

"Why would a whale's tooth set off the metal detector?" Beamish was not convinced.

"Maybe it's a defective detective." His wife snapped.

"There's more to this than meets the eye." Beamish declared, ignoring her.

"Well, you have about twenty minutes 'til lunch to figure it out Sherlock Holmes." She clucked, heading back to her domain, the kitchen.

"It may be a whale's tooth, but I found *this* inside." Beamish announced proudly a few minutes later, as he tracked sand across her just mopped floor.

"Looks like a boardwalk game token to me." The wife replied, unimpressed. "Good for three points at the skee ball redemption center on Seaside Pier. Congratulations. Now all you need is ten million more to get yourself a water pistol."

"Hardeharhar." Beamish countered, in his best Ralph Kramden voice. "Took your tonic this morning and feeling pretty clever aren't you? No, this is a coin all right. Craftmanship's too fine for it to be just a slug or something. I never saw anything like it. There's some sort of foreign language on it. Latin or Spanish maybe. I think it's a doubloon or one of those coins they used to make pieces of eight out of." Beamish had no idea what a 'piece of eight' was. "Wouldn't it be something if it was one of those Brasher Doubloons from American Revolution times. Worth over a million dollars."

"And I'm telling you it's from one of the boardwalk games and if you bite into it, even with *your* bad teeth, all you'll get is a mouthful of tin foil."

"No Evelyn." Beamish persisted, uttering her name with a seriousness that snapped her to attention. "This is gold. I tested it. It's gold I tell you. The detector acted goofy when I passed over it on the beach. Now I gotta figure out how gold finds its way into a whale's tooth."

...One day, for a lark, Captain Kidd ordered his men to lower away a small skiff. He wanted to have a closer look at this whale that had chosen his ship to be its soul mate. If Kidd was nothing else, he was intrepid; fearing neither man nor beast and eager to avoid but one confrontation in this life: with the hangman's noose. He rowed out alone to meet the great monster.

His encounter took place before the birth of Herman Melville so there was no one to document its anticlimactic ending. Kidd helped himself to the Jersey shore's first souvenir as he hacked out a tooth with his cutlass. Kidd laughed and shook his head at the docility of this giant creature impassively riding the waves, allowing the pirate to take such a liberty without taking angry offense. Kidd wondered if the whale realized, as Kidd realized, that the whale could easily destroy the pirate with one casual swipe of his powerful flukes.

Kidd held the tooth to the sun and marveled at the size and ivory whiteness of the thing. Suddenly, the whale's tooth gave Kidd an idea. Chuckling, he flourished his plumed hat at his crew and, already forming a plan, hurried back to his ship...

Beamish played with the whale's tooth that entire afternoon. Sometimes, he stared at the tooth. Sometimes, he eyeballed the coin. Sometimes he placed them side by side on the work bench and, resting his head on his elbows, silently looked at them simultaneously through his magnifying glass, as if hoping to telepathically extract their secrets. Beamish had all the time in the world and for once, he was glad.

Late afternoon, he emerged from the workshop and headed for his car.

"Where ya goin'?" Evelyn asked, half-interested. She assumed he was off on one his regular trips to the local hardware store to pester them for washers or screws or nuts or some other doodad he needed for one of his countless "projects". "Better them than me." She grumbled, returning to her housework with a cluck of pity for the unfortunate clerks at Home Depot.

But Beamish wasn't going to the hardware store. He was headed into unfamiliar territory that would take him to the one place he hadn't visited since he was a school kid, having no need as a level-headed adult for the "impracticalities" they offered. That place was the library. He mused that he'd be turning up in other improbable locales before he was through. Beamish was on a treasure hunt.

...Kidd did not trust his crew. No pirate captain with any longevity in that specialized field of endeavor ever did. Fortunately, none of the crew knew how to read and weren't likely acquainted with anyone possessing that useless skill. Even so, Kidd was pretty cautious about keeping a journal. He was sly in his entries, not wishing to give anyone who happened to be literate and lucky enough to happen upon the journal too clear an idea of where he was hiding his loot. He also had no wish of leaving an incriminating record in his own hand, for a judge to peruse while deliberating on whether to hang a rascal.

Kidd had a prodigious ego, which usually overruled any notion of discretion. He gave full vent to that ego in his scribblings.

Beamish learned about Captain Kidd and his pirate antics in south Jersey's waters during his stop at the library. He formed a grudging respect for a rascal who was very accomplished in his rascality. Kidd had literally terrorized the eastern seaboard for years.

"What if this whale's tooth is connected with pirates?" Beamish speculated.

His long dominant practical nature instantly over ruled that bit of romantic nonsense but there was an unfamiliar tingle running along Beamish spine as he stared long and hard at the tooth. Considering the empty space before his eyes that, at that moment, served as a metaphor for what remained of his life, Beamish decided to believe that the tooth and its gold piece filling and Captain Kidd, real or fanciful, were linked together with all links leading to buried treasure!

Through his readings of the pirate's exploits in those few remaining fragments of his journal and other documents from that era, Beamish was able to utilize his own mechanical genius for constructing workable units from disparate pieces and fragments and cobbled together the first treasure map he'd dealt with since the daydreamy days of his boyhood.

He felt sheepish holding the map. He knew it was foolishness. There was no treasure. There were no heavy chests groaning with gold and precious gems from around the globe. There were no skeletons with bony fingers pointing the way to the next bloodcurdling clue. It was fantasy, child's play, a waste of time.

But if the world of grown-ups no longer needed him to act like a man and work like a man; he would become a child, entertain the fantasies of a child and waste as much time as he had left. Beamish was ready to devote all of the single-minded stubbornness that had gotten him successfully through life to this disconcerting and anticlimactic stage of retirement to get to the metal hard bottom of a legend.

...Alone in his cabin, Kidd held the whale's tooth over a bowl of cement that he'd had prepared that afternoon. The mate had been puzzled at the order, but having sailed with the pirate for a lifetime spanning almost two years, knew better than to question the order or speak of it to the others...silence being an understood part of the order.

Kidd dipped the tooth in cement with a pair of tongs he kept about for other less savory diversions. He held the object long enough for it to fill the tooth's cavity. Then, he took two coins and carefully scratched a series of numbers, location markings. He stuffed one of the coins into the hardening mass. The whale's tooth, Kidd had decided, would serve as first of a number of markers he would place that would later lead him back to his hidden treasure once the nuisance of pursuit from the British fleet had ebbed. The coins, he chuckled, were just one more example of his talent for flair.

There was a sandbar just to the north of the mouth of De La War Bay. This tiny spit of an island housed a small freshwater lake that Kidd had used to replenish his ship's casks in the past. Kidd planned to row ashore that night and arrange his markers and bury the treasure. He figured on taking the mate along and *arrange and bury* him as well. Next day, he planned on engaging a particularly troublesome frigate in battle. Then it was off to the islands where he would live and reign as a king among a nation of adoring and servile natives.

His crew, he would leave to its own inadequate devices...

Beamish map was more of a collage of disparate objects, murky clues, and unspecified locations, most of which no longer existed. It didn't matter. Beamish didn't care if he actually found anything when he finally turned up the x-marked spot he was seeking. The thrill of the quest and the mere fact of once again actually having something to do, filled him with an eagerness to get out of bed each morning that had been lacking since he'd embarked upon this blissful adventure of retirement.

From his research, Beamish was able to deduce that the whale's tooth was the first in a series of direction guides, laid out by Captain Kidd and decipherable only by him, that would lead him to his buried treasure whenever he came calling for it. It took a great deal of guess work and inference to arrive at various conclusions and, almost more than the quest itself, the discovery that he possessed any intuitive abilities after a lifetime of allowing them to atrophy, surprised and further stimulated Beamish.

Beamish learned that there had been a freshwater lake almost dead center of Point Pleasure Island that had nourished a thick grove of magnolia and cedar trees. The tooth, Beamish conjectured, had been placed in what was for Kidd a recognizable spot, to point in the general direction of this lake. Beamish was able to approximate the location of the lake and so noted on his map.

From the descriptions he'd read in the library, Beamish learned that the lake had been lovely, frequented by swans and all sorts of migrating wildlife, especially birds and butterflies. There was also a dazzling variety of colorful wildflowers, vines, and thickets of honeysuckle and rhododendron, low-lying shrubbery around the lake, dense enough for a pirate to use for the concealment of treasure.

It had been *too* dense to suit the settlers who came later, however.

At the turn of the last century, an enterprising developer from the Vineland area had purchased the lake and all the land surrounding the lake. Legend has it that the purchase price from the farmer who had owned it and found the land to be useless for agricultural purposes, had been a sufficient length of calico for his wife to sew a few dresses for herself and their daughters, and a new fangled contraption called an automobile that the farmer could drive up and down the nearby beach whenever the mood to move pointlessly fast came over him.

The developer immediately filled the lake, knocked down all but a few of the trees, tore out the vines and wildflowers, and laid out a sequence of thirty by a hundred foot rectangular building lots interwoven with a grid of connecting streets. The birth of Point Pleasure. As more and more people discovered the advantages of summer visits to the shore, a new form of vegetation blossomed densely across the island: the tourist. And the Borough of Point Pleasure was incorporated and grew, uprooting every remaining tree and blade of grass on the island to make room for more paying occupants.

A man who had always advocated progress and held firmly the belief in man's dominion over everything else on the planet as decreed by the Bible, Beamish nevertheless found himself inexplicably saddened by the loss of the lake and the trees that he'd never seen except in the words of history and a few faded black and white photographs.

He became a positive Earth Firster when he arrived at the place he'd calculated to be the location of the former lake and found instead, the Magnolia

Hotel, a ramshackle five story boarding house that contained a goodly percentage of the island's least reputable residents. The sweet smell of burning marijuana wafted to his nostrils as he entered the lobby, a room marked by stained and peeling wallpaper, several pieces of cheap stick furniture much of which had been rendered back to its original state, a collapsed sofa bed, and three squalling youngsters in diapers who were in competition to see which could get the filthiest. A woman of indeterminate age, wearing her long greasy hair tied back in a bun, ignored the youngsters as well as Beamish; being just then engrossed in the proceedings of that day's edition of the "Jerry Springer Show".

"Just a minute." She huffed indifferently, hanging onto the sordid story unfolding on the television screen until the commercial break. She doubted that Beamish was a customer, that species being a rarity in these parts. She figured him for DYFS or perhaps a minister. He was too old to be a cop, with most of whom she enjoyed a first name relationship.

The woman eyed Beamish impassively as he explained his purpose in visiting. While he spoke, two youths approached and asked him for spare change. Rather than risk confrontation, Beamish emptied his pockets. Pirates may be gone but their descendants are alive and well, Beamish mused. After several futile attempts to communicate with the woman, who addressed him with incoherent mutters, Beamish asked for permission to look in the back yard. His hostess shrugged and turned away, Jerry Springer having returned to the screen to interview a couple of boisterous individuals who turned out to be former friends of the woman and non-paying tenants of the Magnolia Hotel.

Beamish next encountered a pair of men loitering about his car.

"Nice wheels man." One observed in unaccented yet broken English. The other nodded. Beamish eyed them uneasily but, seeing his doors locked, he proceeded into the yard. Recalling the description of the place as having been thick with honeysuckle, vines, and wildflowers, he felt impotent rage when he encountered the culmination of what human progress had created.

Scorched earth. Every blade of grass, every lowly weed, anything suggesting life, had been crushed and trampled by indifferent feet. Fences and walls divided properties into compounds, each of which boasted a yard in similar condition. In the far corner of this ShangriLa, these people who couldn't take care of themselves, had insisted upon keeping a number of dogs penned in clearly undersized cages. If this ground did yield a crop, it was the accumulated droppings of these mistreated creatures.

Beamish was no PETA sympathizer but the condition of these dogs made him confrontational. He stormed out of the yard, passing the two men who had already removed one and were busily liberating a second of his tires. Beamish raced into the hotel lobby and raising his voice above the music of the youth choir and the hysterics of Jerry Springer et al, caught the undivided attention of the slovenly concierge who promptly laid him out with a lead pipe kept conveniently under the counter for those frequent occasions when someone got out of hand.

Next thing he knew, Beamish was sitting in the back seat of a police squad car for the first time in his life.

"They won't press charges if you don't say anything about your car." A voice advised him through the grate.

"What about my car?" Beamish asked, shaking out the cobwebs.

His car, or what remained of it, was still where he'd parked it. The tires were missing. The trunk had been pried open and its contents, including his metal detector, were gone.

"Funny, they didn't take the radio. You must have surprised them." The cop deduced. "What were you doing there anyway?"

Beamish groaned, felt foolish, and then reluctantly told the policemen his story.

"Lake around here. Huh? Pirate treasure. Well, if there's any treasure, you can bet that rat's nest of pirates would've dug it up by now. They can smell unearned money ten miles away." One officer observed, not without a trace of admiration.

"Say, why don't you stop by the Point Pleasure Hall of Fame." His partner quickly interjected. "Don't they have some old stuff up there?"

"I didn't know the town had its own museum. I've been working out at the county library on this." Beamish wondered.

"Ain't exactly a museum. More like a room full of old things nobody wants anymore." The cop explained. "They tried to get a museum started here but no one wanted to do any volunteer work so all the stuff just sorta sits up in a room on the second floor of Borough Hall."

"Anything there from the lake?" Beamish asked.

"I remember when they tore down the old Hoffman house, he had some kind of tree that used to be the town symbol before they changed the name to Point Pleasure. That's up there."

"A tree!" Beamish exclaimed. "You're not talking about the M tree. Largest, oldest tree on the island, a book said. Grew right at the edge of the lake. Hung its thickest branches out over the water. One long crooked branch shaped itself into the letter 'M'."

"I'll be dammed." The cop exclaimed, catching Beamish's excitement. "I remember something. They used to call this island Magnolia Grove. Held community meetings, weddings, christenings…all sorts of public events, under that tree. Never heard anything about pirates or treasure, though."

Beamish shook his head. He wasn't certain but, from the bits and pieces he was able to put together, it's possible that captain Kidd had paid a secret visit to the Magnolia tree one night, ages ago. Beamish asked to be taken to Borough Hall.

…There was no light for miles other than that offered by a pale moon and a skyful of twinkling stars, on the night Captain Kidd and his mate stealthily rowed to shore on a barrier island along a desolate stretch of coast south of New York. The rest of the crew, fortified with an extra ration of rum, slept the sleep of the righteously drunken.

Kidd lit a torch and peered into the darkness, commanding the mate to follow.

Using his instruments and the stars, Kidd took some navigational readings, then trudged inland through the sand for some time, before pausing again.

"Dig here." He commanded. "Twenty hands deep."

As the mate toiled in the dark, Kidd stared out to sea. My time will soon be over, he thought, squinting into the inky depths of the night mingled sea. Time to prepare for another kind of life. Kidd was not certain what he'd actually meant by that, His musings were interrupted by the mate who had completed his task. Kidd stepped forward and inspected the hole.

"Good. Very good." He said in a calm voice. The mate glanced up at his captain in time to see the butt end of the cutlass that crushed his skull. "Good. Very good." Kidd repeated as the mate's lifeless form crumpled at his feet. "No need to bury you on this sand bar, my loyal shipmate. What the sea doesn't take, the sharks will. None but you and I will ever be the wiser."

He dragged the mate down to the water's edge and watched him tumble away in the frothing surf.

Returning briskly to his business, Kidd returned to the hole. There, he removed an object from his pocket and gingerly placed it in the hole. Careful to position it so that it pointed toward a certain spot in the center of the island, near the lake. He cursed, when he realized that he should have waited for the mate to refill the hole before disposing of him. With a shrug, he set to work filling and smoothing the sand until the area looked as undisturbed as the rest of the universe at what had transpired that night. But having taken meticulous readings which he committed to memory, Kidd was confident he could find the spot blind folded at midnight on the darkest, evilest night Hell could conjure.

The pirate hoisted two large chests onto either shoulder, and trudged upland toward a thick stand of trees around this pleasant little lake he knew quite well…

The receptionist, a gum snapping youngster fresh out of receptionist school, sat at her desk in the middle of the Borough hall lobby and looked at Beamish like he'd just gotten off the express shuttle from Mars. She didn't have a clue as to what he was referring when he asked for directions to the museum. She turned testy when he suggested she ask someone and downright surly when he requested to speak with anyone with any kind of authority.

This request instigated the dolorous weave of the bureaucracy's chain of command directly about Beamish's neck. If anything, the summoned supervisor was testier and surlier in imperiously announcing that there was no museum in Borough hall and never had been in the thirty-one years she'd labored in that place. Beamish, no slouch in the obnoxiousness department, suggested that if the supervisor had ever put aside her personal phone calls and donuts long enough to take a stroll around the building, she might actually learn what else shared that building with her.

That brought the security guard into the picture. A retired longshoreman from Philadelphia, he happened to know what Beamish was talking about and, eager for something to finally do, volunteered to escort Beamish upstairs to the place in question.

"Oh you mean the old storage room. That's no museum." The supervisor said, suddenly becoming a wealth of information. "That's just a storeroom full of useless junk."

"No madam," Beamish concluded, tapping his skull and indicating her own, "*that* is an old store room full of useless junk."

However, the supervisor's assessment was close to the mark, Beamish learned as he waded and climbed through piles of broken copier and fax machines, disconnected telephones, discarded desk chairs and other flotsam and jetsam from the arduous world of modern work. Finally, he reached a corner of the room in which huddled a few of the remaining relics of what had once been the island's preserved history.

Beamish looked for the tree, knowing already that it could not still be alive in this dark and dusty place where machinery went to die. He clucked as he sifted among the broken parts of gadgets that he could easily fix with a handful of washers, screws, pliers and wrench, and about a quarter mile of electrical tape. A room full of loot, discarded by heedless bureaucrat types who, having no skill or inclination to repair, simply buried and went out to get more.

"My tax dollars at work." Beamish fumed. "Who says there are no longer any pirates?"

He spotted it then. He didn't want it to be the thing he was seeking but it couldn't be anything else. Apparently uprooted long ago when its presence impeded the march of progress, the tree had been "replanted" in a wide and shallow barrel. Or at least some fragment of it had. Looking at the skeleton in the corner, Beamish could not imagine this as the largest tree on the island; could not envision it in its glory of massive limbs dangling playfully over Magnolia lake as it shot branches skyward at every angle conceivable.

It was dead, bleached whiter and deader than any sea scoured piece of driftwood. The 'M' shape had been whittled down by time and indifference until what was left resembled some perverse wooden sculpture (resembling the arches logo of the fast food chain that now occupied a spot near its former location) one would find in some two bit souvenir shop on the road leading onto the island.

There were plenty of clues about what had happened to this island to be read in this decayed stick, but no tale of pirate treasure, Beamish thought angrily. He could not hear wedding bells or the cries of newborn babies impatient to be named. Instead, he felt the uniqueness of a place destroyed, its history hacked away in the name of profit, neglected in the name of expediency and finally entombed out of sight, out of mind; kept to satisfy some faint echo of guilt and stashed among all the other accumulated detritus of modern life. All the old secrets lost, all connections to the past broken.

"What have you done!" Beamish shouted. "What have we all done!"

The use of the verb 'do' in this hallowed shrine of inertia, brought curious bureaucrats out of their form induced comas. Many actually looked out of their cubicles, some long dormant sense of curiosity aroused. The City Manager, confused that someone was rummaging about in the store room, entered, followed by his executive assistant, two administrative aides, three junior g-men, and four calling birds.

"What are you doing here?" he demanded, keeping a distance.

"Do you have authorization?" the chorus sang.

"You let it die." Beamish accused.

"We let nothing die. What are you talking about?" the manager asked crisply, motioning a clerk typist to summon the police before turning back to Beamish and assuming his smooth unflappable professional voice. "Suppose you come out of there and we'll discuss this in my office?"

"Why? So you can give me forms to complete in quadruplicate that some snotty kid will run copies of before she breaks the machine because she doesn't have enough sense to unclog a paper jam?"

"Please come out, we don't want you to get hurt."

"No, you don't want me to sue. Because if I fall in here, I *could* sue. This equipment isn't supposed to be kept this way. There are all sorts of flammable and toxic materials in this unventilated room."

The manager frowned. A lunatic was one thing. A lunatic who knew something that could come back to hurt the manager was another.

"If you come out now, no charges will be filed." He bluffed.

"For what? Visiting the city museum? That's what this room is officially listed as. Open to the public. Check your records, if you can find a filing cabinet you can open."

The police arrived just then.

"*You* again" the cop from the Magnolia House laughed. "Getting to be quite the public enemy number one. Please step out here and we'll straighten out this mess, sir."

"It'll take years to straighten out this mess." Beamish gestured around him. "And how long will it take to regrow that tree?"

"Please remain calm and no one will get hurt." The police entered the room, moving slowly toward Beamish on either side.

Suddenly, Beamish snapped off one the 'M' tree's remaining limbs and brandished it like a sword in the faces of the policemen.

"You'll never take me alive!" He cackled.

Beamish attempted to swing over his assailants by grabbing hold to an overhead hanging ceiling light. The cops started laughing at the sight of the old man doing an Errol Flynn impression. But when Beamish gave one of the uniforms a hearty smack with the branch, they became all business again. Beamish swung his sword again. This time, he broke it across the back of the city manager, who quickly fled from the room. Then, an entire platoon of aides, file clerks, typists, and other functionaries stormed the room and brought the flailing Beamish to the floor.

As the dust literally settled, Beamish heard a metallic clang as something shiny fell out of the broken tree branch. In the confusion, he was able to pocket the object. He knew exactly what it was.

...Having frequented the place in the past, Kidd had no difficulty threading the narrow Indian path leading inland to the lake. He methodically hacked away at over–growths of poison ivy, honeysuckle, and bayberry until he reached the higher ground where magnolia trees circled about the lake. Knowing the particular tree he was seeking, he squinted through the utter darkness until he made out its distinctive silhouette, rising above its fellows.

Kidd rubbed the sturdy limbs of the tree until he found the spot he was seeking. Then taking his knife, he cut a deep gash and inserted his marker He covered the gash with mud and bark as best he could. That done, he shouldered his chests and headed further upland into the marshes to hide more clues and, finally, the chests themselves.

Kidd never made a return trip to that sand bar. Several days after his night visit to the island, his ship encountered a British man o'war that had been stalking him along the coast. There was a fierce but brief battle and Kidd was taken. He was returned to England, where he was tried and hanged. Legend has it that Kidd was so tough that the hangman failed in his assignment the first time and William Kidd had to be hanged twice.

No trace was ever found of the clues he'd left that would lead to the chests he'd hidden...

It didn't matter to Beamish that he didn't find the treasure or even learn the meaning of the coins he'd found. After he'd been arrested for the first time in his life and Evelyn had posted bail and the charges were dropped, a profound change came over Beamish.

It wasn't peace, exactly. It wasn't surrender to the inevitable. But it was obvious that Beamish had resolved an inner conflict of long standing as a result of his treasure hunt.

He no longer hid himself away for hours on end; tinkering in the garage. He passed more time out of doors; especially on the beach. His walks to the beach were different. He went gadgetless. He no longer bundled himself against the elements; choosing instead to breathe in deeply, savoring each breath as though it were his last. His beach walks no longer had a mercenary purpose. Now, he'd linger longer and longer at the sea's edge and look thoughtfully toward the horizon.

Beamish felt a greater appreciation for the tenacious dune grass that defied wind and sea to hang on precariously by roots deeply entrenched in the sand. He noted the sandpipers that, day after day, trudged along the tide line poking about for the tiny crustaceans that composed their daily fare. Beamish developed a sense of camaraderie with all the plants and animals hardy enough to endure and thrive in such an inhospitable place.

One warm Spring day, a mother sunned herself on the beach while her two young boys dug in the sand down near water's edge. Beamish paused to watch discreetly and overheard the boys playing pirate. Using pieces of washed up driftwood for swords, the boys dug ferociously, expecting to find something; only to be disappointed when all they uncovered was more sand.

Beamish reached into his coat pocket and found two gold coins that had once sent him off blindly seeking treasures left over from a time and place that no longer existed. He buried the coins with the toe of his shoe. Pretending that he was sharing a great secret, he advised the boys where to dig. He laughed and shook his head knowingly when the boys, instead of sharing the loot they found, fought a fierce sword battle to determine who would get to keep it all. The mother sunned herself, oblivious the whole time.

That afternoon, Beamish received a call from Point Pleasure Police Department.

"Mr. Beamish, we recovered your metal detector. If you'd like to come down to the station to identify it and complete some paperwork, we'll be happy to return it to you." An official voice advised.

"No officer." Beamish laughed good-naturedly. "Keep it. Better yet, put in the museum with the tree and the rest of the town's unwanted treasures. Keep it there as a symbol of man's tendency to look for treasures in all the wrong places and in all the wrong ways."

With that thought fresh in his mind, Beamish headed toward the kitchen to pester his wife.

"Point Pleasure Odyssey"

Nicky's journey home to Point Pleasure actually started before the day he left the island. Like many men his age, old enough to know better, not old enough to accept that knowledge, he became involved with the wrong woman. There was never going to be a right time or a right place to be involved with this woman. But the result of Nicky's involvement was that his heir now walked the earth, unwanted and unrecognized by his father

Responsibility is thrust upon a man at a pivotal point in life. In Nicky's case, the test had been presented and he had responded less than heroically.

Not feeling bound by time-honored traditions of family and manhood that had been passed down through his family's bloodlines for centuries, Nicky stole from his family and ran away with the woman before he abandoned her and, without knowing it or caring, his heir.

The best that can be said for the child is that it passes quickly from this story, without ever knowing its father. It would grow up in a void of sorts but a void is far easier to negotiate than an obstacle.

A void can be passed through. An obstacle must be overcome. In the troubled person of Nicky, the fates had knitted together a formidable obstacle indeed, for anyone attempting to untangle the webs of whim and caprice in which a person can ensnare himself.

The family patriarch was a hard man who had made his way in the New World by grit and determination and had risen in the ranks of Point Pleasure to be a scion of the local economy. He had tried disciplining his son in the past when he misstepped but the son had always wormed himself back into his good graces. His behavior this time required a sterner measure, an 'act of tough love' intended to teach a lesson and bring a beloved, wayward child back into the family fold once and for all or lose him.

His father banished him from his bayside palace with the admonition that he could not come home until he learned how to behave like a man.

Nicky had always weaseled back into the old man's good graces through his mother, who could not long tolerate life without her only son and favorite child. For a young man of Nicky's talents and disposition, birth into a wealthy family had been a stroke of good fortune.

First generation American first born son of Greek immigrants, Nicky had been given everything and worked for nothing thanks to these parents, who'd come off the boat with nothing, save the stars in their eyes and the willingness to work for everything. The pinnacle of their success assumed the form of this son.

Nicky's parents had started their American success story with a small boardwalk concession, a fast food joint that, like so many other Greek immigrant-owned fast food joints on the Point Pleasure boardwalk; sold the usual burgers and hot beef sandwiches along with exotic-sounding but actually pedestrian items like gyros and souvlakis. Their wares were advertised by hanging large slabs of beef suspended over heating trays in the front of the stand facing the boardwalk. The idea was to entice strollers; presumably anyone noticing these slabs of meat would be overcome with hunger.

Their first summer, Nicky's parents neglected to change that slab of meat until mid-August; when someone representing the local health department indelicately suggested that they should try serving up some of the huge well-fed flies that lingered in number on the premises.

But they learned the ropes quickly. Like most immigrants, they were hard-working and thrifty people who truly believed in the premise of the American Dream.

After two seasons, they were able to open a second, larger restaurant. After the third season, they bought both buildings so the lion's share of their earnings would no longer go to an absentee landlord.

Nicky was born that happy third winter. The family had been accepted into what passed for an off-season community in Point Pleasure. Nicky's father, a proud man of old world manners and morals, took his new-found position seriously. He became deeply involved in community matters. Helping to lay the foundations for the area's first Greek Orthodox Church, for example.

Business continued to be his main concern. After another successful summer, he acquired Sunrise Pier, a dilapidated former fishing pier at the north end of the boardwalk; so named because it was the first man-made structure on the island to greet the sun as it rose out of the Atlantic each morning.

"You can almost see Apollo's golden chariot." Nicky's father would joke, holding his son high in the sky as he shared his allusions to ancient Greek culture. For though the man had worked hard to make himself an American, he retained a fascination for the ancient mythology of home; a scholarly interest he'd retained from youth.

His plans for the pier were to create a sort of mythology theme park. He began his effort by importing a lavish, two tiered carousel from Greece. Instead of horse, the children would ride on the backs of centaurs. A mural depicting a bucolic scene from Mount Olympus served as a rotating backdrop.

In addition to the gem-encrusted, marble and brass carousel, there were more modern rides in concession to the nature of the very competitive amusement business. These had the usual flashing lights, numbing loud sound systems, and body wrenching special effects movements. A wet dream for chiropractors, he'd called them.

Life size, white plaster statues of various characters from antiquity were strategically placed about the pier; guides to the various attractions. The pier also boasted the largest roller coaster to be found in New Jersey.

And then, in the center of it all, he placed the maze.

The maze was a fun house. It was a dark place filled with dim flickering electric candles intended to create the aura of torches in a cave. It was a walk through attraction and a puzzle; to get through the cave, where exotic creatures borrowed from old world lore waited behind various corners and concealed in dark nooks. Slithering Medusan serpents with long razor sharp tails; harpies with claws and fangs bared and ready to rip asunder any mis-stepping wanderer; fire-breathing dragons with red neon eyes ever glaring and snarling Cyclops, one terrible eye beaming out from its cave waiting to snatch the unwary. And among these terrible creatures were the more terrible gods: Zeus, holding a flashing lightning bolt showing the way into the maze; Hercules, holding back moving walls that threaten at any moment to collapse upon the wanderer; Athena, the goddess of wisdom with her all-seeing eye penetrating the darkness to wordlessly guide the wanderer past the Medusa with her horrible face and snakelike hair.

And in the center of the maze, always waiting: the sphinx. Part lion, part woman, always inscrutable; tape recorded voice activated by tripping an infrared light, greeting the wanderer with one of seven riddles. The person correctly answering the riddle was shown the path leading out and earned a stuffed animal prize for successfully navigating the maze. An incorrect answer left the wanderer to find his own way. Eventually a ride attendant would come to the rescue.

As a young boy, Nicky lived the ultimate child's fantasy. He passed summer days and nights roaming the pier while his father oversaw operations from an office overlooking the whole.

However, as the boy grew, the play distractions of boyhood were put aside and Nicky was given responsibility and hard work. He was never coddled by his father. But he was coddled by Point Pleasure in deference to his father's standing in the community.

Even at a young age Nicky showed a talent for getting into trouble. Indiscretions in elementary school became delinquency in high school. In the community, rumors spread of Nicky's affinity for the shadier aspects of life in Point Pleasure. Too many rumors from too many disparate sources over an extended period of time for them to be ignored.

While the father remained adamant in defending his son, he grew more exasperated and less tolerant as time passed.

In high school, Nicky would sneak into the maze after closing; bringing drugs and drinking companions and girls. Usually, their romps in the funhouse ended with trouble as the night watchman chased them. Nicky was never caught. But his father knew.

Nicky finally reached an age when those cold, uneventful Point Pleasure winters no longer suited his mercurial nature. Having finished at Point Pleasure High, he had gone to Fort Lauderdale and attended a nearby community college. But he came home; after one disastrous semester, during which he discovered that his father's influence did not cross state boundaries and the hijinks of adolescence would not be tolerated in one now considered to have entered into manhood.

He cajoled his father into offering still another chance and was installed in the family business. Nicky was given management of the family's original restaurant.

He had no mind for business. He quickly became bored and inattentive. Always more comfortable playing the social butterfly, he even became bored with what passed for social life in off-season Point Pleasure; a culture fueled by copious amounts of drugs and alcohol; steeped in gossip, punctuated by the occasional scandal.

Nicky gravitated to the wrong crowd. His fall from grace came quickly and was a short one.

One quiet, snowy night, Nicky fell from his father's good graces for the last time.

He stole a week's receipts from the restaurant and left town with the hostess.

The patriarch was livid when he learned of the theft. Once again, he pronounced banishment. Not even the tearful pleadings of his wife, who never meddled in these matters, would induce him to relent. This time, the anger and bitter disappointment he felt, broke the old man. He declared, in the presence of his daughter and the family attorney, that his only son was disowned and all his worldly possessions would eventually pass to his daughter and the guy lucky enough to marry her. On that day, as he erased his son from his heart, he began to diminish.

Unaware of this last bridge burning behind him, Nicky returned to the warm climate of Florida without enough money to get him through the balance of that winter.

Florida proved to be more than warm. It grew positively torrid for Nicky after his money ran out. Shortly after, Nicky ran out on the girl. Honest work was as hard to come by there as it was in Point Pleasure in the off season. Not that Nicky was looking for honest work. Employment of the other stripe was to be had in abundance and Nicky found himself utilizing some of his less socially acceptable skills.

Nicky's inclination toward life's tawdrier opportunities once again belied his upbringing. The concept of working hard and aspiring upward was anathema to someone whose parents had done the aspiring and working for him; affording him a birthing room view of the world from the top. No hourly wage jobs for Nicky.

It seemed a perfect fit: Nicky and Florida's thriving illegal narcotics business. But though he was well-known to dealers in the Point Pleasure vicinity, he was an outsider in Florida. His initial venture into this free-wheeling capitalistic enterprise, ended with a back eye, several broken ribs and what developed into a dose of venereal disease, courtesy of two very tough young ladies from South America who rolled him at 3 a.m. after a misunderstanding behind an unsavory bar in Miami.

Nicky, thoroughly beaten, was nonetheless impressed by the sheer economics-based ruthlessness of the girls.

He figured he needed more "educational opportunities" to improve his prospects so he enrolled in a local college. Here, he quickly earned the nickname, "Stash". The nickname catapulted him to local celebrity. His fame quickly spread beyond the ivy-covered halls of Florida academe. Stash came to the attention of both the local police headquarters and the less official HQ of those individuals who had considered the campus their particular "territory".

Another encounter in the wee hours of the pre-sunshine morning in the Sunshine State left Nicky limping, wheezing, and hearing the call to go west. Nicky followed in the footsteps of many a pioneer and, scrounging what money he could, bought a one way bus ticket to the end of the line.

He ended up in Reno, where an old high school buddy worked as a casino pit boss. Nicky sniffed back mucus through nostrils shattered by too much cocaine and too few self defense skills. He hoped his fortunes would change for the better in the midst of the astronomical financial opportunities offered in a gambling-based economy. In any event, the dry air felt good on those nostrils.

Nicky did well in Reno initially. He had a knack for dealing cards. His swarthy good looks made him a favorite with the ladies who frequented his table and were generous with tips. He worked hard, accepting every shift offered, often working doubles.

Having left his taste for booze and cocaine in Florida, Nicky made a new acquaintance in Nevada: amphetamine. In Nicky's lexicon, this was not a drug. Its use served a strictly medical function: it enabled Nicky to stay alert through the double shifts and kept him going at a breakneck pace that at first amazed and eventually concerned his employer.

He increased daily dosages and became more intimately associated with the purveyors of this miracle product. There were all night parties after sixteen hour shifts. There were trips to California and ski weekends in Colorado. There were business visits across the Mexican border. It all became blurred to Nicky until, one day, his old high school buddy informed him that he couldn't cover for him any more.

Nicky saw speed as his edge in Edge City. His employers saw it as an addiction.He was sent to in-house counseling which proved pointless since Nicky was able to rationalize his behavior and never admitted to having any problems.

How dare they criticize me! He raged. He felt above all their criticism. From his Olympian perspective he clearly saw the hypocrisy of his situation: criticizing his "addiction' when day in day out this industry pandered to an even sicker addiction.

He voiced that very opinion, arrogantly righteous, at a disciplinary meeting with the casino manager. It had been the final stage hearing for disciplinary action after a series of write-ups and short suspensions. In his state, Nicky was not even aware that he'd agreed to write-ups of his unacceptable behavior; did not even know that he'd been held out of work without pay for several five day periods.

The manager wasn't sure Nicky even knew what was happening when he handed him his 'final discharge' separation packet. Nor did the manager care.

The fates weren't through with Nicky, not by a long shot. There were still many threads to work into the weave of his life. About the time, Nicky's manager was finishing his discharge paperwork, a number of casino executives defected from Reno to a competitor opening a casino in Atlantic City.

Nicky had shared lines of crystal meth and the affections of a spaced-out cocktail waitress with one of these executives. To enhance their betrayal of their original employer, these managers twisted the knife and gave it a tweak by stealing as many of the company's experienced employees as possible in order to enter Atlantic City with an entourage. Nicky's patron, thinking a change of venue bringing him close to home and into familiar territory, might be just the tonic to wise up the young Greek, arranged for Nicky to return east with the mass exodus from Reno.

"You'll be back with family and friends, the people you grew up around. Places you know.AC is hot now. It's the new frontier." That was how the offer was proposed but in a tone that suggested a fait accompli. Stavros saw the menacing leer behind the magnanimous gesture.

Ashen faced, hands quivering from drug withdraw, eyes bloodshot and downcast, Nicky unsteadily took the next step in his journey. There was no family awaiting him with open arms. No trumpets of fanfare. Any possibility had blotted all of that from the books. Not even drugs could delude him on that score.

Atlantic City was as different from Reno in temperament as it is in terms of geography. Nicky became quickly depressed; with the weather, the marked contrast between the casino world and the rest of the decayed city, the clientele in the casino. The latter tended to be dominated by hordes of Social Security recipients. They came by the busload. You knew when the mailmen brought the monthly checks. The first few days of each month drew crowds to the gaming tables where losses, though comparatively small by Reno standards, assumed cataclysmic proportions for the losers. Even worse were the hard core working class gamblers from nearby east coast cities like New York and Philly who weren't able to afford losing their weekly paychecks. These often took out their disappointments on the dealers.

How much they differed from the easier going crowds out west, Nicky mused.

Nicky curtailed his drug use in Atlantic City. But he rediscovered an old companion, alcohol. Atlantic City was a hard-bitten town; a resort that still recalled its past grandeur as the "playground of the world". The relationship between the new casinos and the rest of Atlantic City was bittersweet. The casinos had promised much, coming in. And they had generated considerable monies in revenues for themselves and government in the form of taxes. The casinos had also created thousands of jobs but many of these jobs had gone to outsiders such as the invaders from Reno.

For locals, the glittering promise had fallen short. Locals felt deceived by the gaudy gaming palaces that had risen up along the ocean front; high above the surrounding squalor; sparkling monuments to man's greed, vanity, and fleeting hopes.

Nicky quickly learned that Atlantic City was steeped in vice; a place where a pinched face malcontent such as himself, could easily find any sort of diversion to temporarily obliterate the pain of life's everyday shabbiness. Nicky sought, and found, his escapes in seedy west side hotel rooms and the back alleys of a number of gloomy bars squatting in forever dark shadows cast by those glittering towers of gold, temples of Midas with that touch that everyone sought to brush against, however briefly.

Nicky was able to stay afloat for a short while in Atlantic City. Booze helped him function in the quick-paced hostility that constituted life there. But he could not elude the inevitable. Luck had not been his strong suit since he'd thumbed his nose at that lady in squandering the good fortune of his birth. Once again, his superiors at work noticed quirks that became counseling issues and finally irreconcilable problems.

Inevitably, Nicky was fired for reporting to work in an obviously intoxicated state. He did not protest the decision to terminate him. He simply shrugged, explained that he'd gotten his days mixed up and by the time he realized he was scheduled to work, had already commenced drinking. He received no sympathy. He then attempted to punch his supervisor, which led to his being unceremoniously escorted from the premises by three burly security officers. Such was the indifference felt by the industry toward Nicky that no charges were filed.

Nicky squandered his meager savings over the ensuing weeks. Just one more tequila, one more line of coke; Nicky reasoned, and he would break through that inhibiting tangle that the fates had woven about him. He might at last escape the aura of bad luck that had enveloped him. That single idea became an obsession as well as a rationalization. Someone up there (finger pointed at some unseen Olympus, inside a casino penthouse.) had it in for him.

But he consoled himself, his time was coming. Just wait. Have another drink. The tables will turn.

The tables did not turn. Once during a three day debauch, Nicky enjoyed a lucid moment and realized that he'd been running ever since he'd fled his home. He had devoted a lion's share of his energies and resources to the process of fleeing.

Out of work and physically wasted from his excesses, he saw that he could not continue much longer this way. His apartment rent was long past overdue and the landlord was in daily contact with the police who were interested in talking to Nicky on unrelated business. Since he'd blackballed himself at the only "industry" in Atlantic City, his employment prospects were nil.

The fates are inscrutable but usually their patterns are obvious. Their impeccable needlework in weaving the intricate interconnected threads of life, created a pattern that formed an undeniably complete mosaic. Nicky had come full circle. He would return to his place of origin. He would come back to Point Pleasure.

He barely managed to scrape together enough change for bus fare. He would not dare to contact the family that had disowned him. Though it occasionally weighed upon him that he brought disgrace upon them, time had sufficiently healed his wounded psyche so that now he could see *himself* as the wronged party. He managed to get his shaking hands around the neck of a cheap bottle of rye whiskey, his companion for the bus ride south.

Two hours later, Nicky staggered drunkenly out of the Point Pleasure bus depot which was deserted this time of year except for a lounging gypsy cab driver. Nicky took a look at Point Pleasure after an odyssey of less than three years that had seemed to be three lifetimes. No festive crowds or fatted calves were on hand to greet him.

Drunk, yet instinctively afraid of being recognized in that state in his hometown, Nicky kept to dark and empty side streets as he made his way to the only place that might afford him temporary refuge until he decided his next move. Harvey's house.

Harvey was a relative by marriage. How a non-Greek like Harvey had managed to penetrate the close-knit Greek world was a saga in itself. The details were a blur to Nicky. In fact, he wasn't exactly sure who Harvey had married. But Harvey had been the only member of the family who had not abandoned him. They had played together on the Point Pleasure High School basketball team. Anyone hailing from a small town understands how lasting such a bond is.

Nicky remembered that, long after the glory of their high school years had faded, they played ball every Tuesday night at the rec center. Two on two games, usually against current crops of pretenders to their various school records. After each such encounter, they'd sit on Harvey's front porch and drink beer and remember girls and inflate past glories.

Harvey would remember. Harvey would help him.

Harvey was out when Nicky came calling, unannounced. Nicky assumed that Harvey had gone out with whichever relative it was he'd married. A light was on in the living room. The lamp in the window welcoming the wandering hero home.

Nicky found an unlocked window on the side of the house. He imagined their reunion. Harvey comes home to find Nicky waiting in the guest seat of honor. The wine would flow. Adventures would be recalled. Tales would be told into the wee hours of morning. Climbing in unsteadily, Nicky kicked over the lamp. He entered the house in darkness.

He managed to navigate to the liquor cabinet where he liberated a bottle. Smacking his lips, he took a long, desperately needed pull. Vodka. Then, he flopped on Harvey's couch and awaited his old friend's return.

Harvey found Nicky curled up on the sofa, cradling the bottle. It took some time for Harvey to recognize his old courtmate. Having recognized him, it took longer for Harvey to believe that this deteriorated bag of bones; with his unwashed clothes, unkempt hair, and dirty unshaven face, was the same proud clean and healthy future hope of an aspiring immigrant family.

Harvey was both moved to pity and disgusted. He let Nicky sleep off his drunk. Next afternoon, Nicky finally awoke, embarrassed and disoriented. Harvey wordlessly handed him a $20 bill and not so subtly directed him to the door. Harvey was unable to conceal his loathing for what Nicky had become. Seeing that look on his old friend's face, Nicky offered no protest and understood that there would be no grand reunion celebration. He took the $20.

He had reached rock bottom. Nowhere to go, nothing to do, no one wondering what had become of him. Nicky wandered to the west side of Point Pleasure, to the harbor where the fishing fleet docked. Actually, Point Pleasure's fleet was a shadow of its former glory, now reduced to perhaps a dozen mostly rust-rotted boats. About a third of these were sea-worthy on a calm day.

Idle fishermen could usually be found passing the time at waterfront bars, dark smoke-filled dens, reeking of urine, vomit, and an indifference calcified from years of testimony to the harshness of a lifestyle trying to sustain itself long after it had been rendered superfluous. Here, beer and whiskey flowed as copiously as the blood spilled in violent encounters between dinosaurs too stupefied to realize they're extinct.

The twenty dollars was used up quickly. So was the good will it had briefly purchased from the loafers who'd befriended him as long as the drink flowed. Friend just as easily assumed the role of foe. A deadly battle ensued with Nicky catching the worse of it. He was left bloodied and motionless in an alley, reeking of menhaden and squid and fouler juices.

There, Nicky passed the second night of his homecoming.

Nicky thought he had managed to return to Point Pleasure without that fact coming to the attention of his family. In that, too, he was self-deluded. His whereabouts were reported every minute of the day. The family was curious to see how Nicky handled himself on his own. Also, the family wanted to know his whereabouts so as to maintain their distance from him. The family was especially desirous of protecting an ailing mother.

His return home had been so dispiriting that Nicky felt compelled to keep himself intoxicated in order to hold off that shrill harpy, despair. An unforgiving sun greeted Nicky in the morning, casting barbs of revealing light through his desiccated soul. But there would be no illumination. The sun slipped behind a cloud. Nicky, too weak in the knees to stand, covered his head.

There was no moral straw to the story for Nicky to grasp. He did not know how to be self-analytical. He was defiant in his refusal to acknowledge the need for self scrutiny. He clung to the notion that he was a victim of a series of events that fate had strung together to torment him. The fact that he had succumbed in each instance eluded him.

Nicky could never see the pattern. All he saw was unfairness and personal hardship. He had come home. He had followed the thread through a labyrinth filled with all sorts of dangerous situations and had made it home. But now that he was home, he saw no noble conclusion to his tragedy.

Perhaps a drink might help clear up his thinking. That was the best solution his muddled brain could come up with.

What he needed was money. He visited the one spot all year round residents of seasonal tourist towns know quite well in the off season: the unemployment office.

On his first visit, Nicky was handed a thick packet of forms and was curtly told to return the following day, forms completed.

That night, Nicky crumpled the packet of forms and used them as a pillow as he slept under the boardwalk. A cheap bottle of wine and a few stray pigeons were his companions.

Shortly after sunrise, he was rousted by the police. He thought he recognized the face of an old high school buddy. There was no return flicker of recognition and he was coldly advised to move on.

Having superficially bathed at a public restroom on the boardwalk, Nicky appeared at the unemployment office. A clerk imperious scanned his soiled paperwork.

"You were fired." She informed him.

He nodded as timidly.

"You can't collect if you're fired, hon." She continued, addressing him as the simpleton she assumed him to be.

"What should I do?" he asked.

"That's *your* problem. I'll schedule you to talk with an examiner. Next opening is three weeks from tomorrow."

"But I need money *now*." Three weeks was an eternity.

"I can't do anything about that, hon. We've got rules and procedures to follow. That's how it goes."

"Is there anyone I can talk to?"

"Sure. The examiner. In three weeks. NEXT!"

Nicky's head hurt. He wasn't sure if it was from lack of drink or from butting heads with the bureaucracy. He had no money; no where to go. He was at the edge of the continent and the cold Atlantic lashed up against the jetties. That night, he returned to the Underwood Motel.

The Underwood Motel had gotten its name from generations of drifters, coming through Point Pleasure seeking summer employment, who turned out to be less than spectacular participants in the economic system. Over the years, a small city had evolved in the dark shadows under the amusement piers, behind tangles of wild growth vines and the accumulated trash and unwanted and expendable surplus of the tourist system playing out overhead.

Nicky noticed a jigsaw puzzle of old cardboard appliance boxes and vegetable and milk crates ticktacked together; the entire cobbling comprising a seven room luxury underwood condo. Being designed for warmer weather, the structure was now deserted; its occupant rousted by the police during one of their random beach sweeps, inspired by the expressed indignation of some sore-headed good citizen merchant type who didn't want to see anybody else get by for nothing "when I'm paying all these taxes…"

A good citizen like Nicky's father.

As Nicky assumed occupancy and curled up inside his cardboard bedroom, he recalled the last time he'd ventured under the boardwalk. He was in high school and it was his senior prom. He'd come under the boards after a moonlight dip with his date, the daughter of a prominent local attorney who doubled as assistant coach for the basketball team. There was champagne...only the best for Nicky in those days.

The girl had resisted at first but that had been for show. The wine and the moon and hormones conspired in Nicky's favor. He winced now as he recalled how a few years later that same girl, now head hostess in the family restaurant he was running, announced that she was pregnant and he was the father. That indiscretion had started the fates weaving their threads that had come together in the noose Nicky now observed dangling from a rafter of the Underwood Motel. Left by coincidence by an unhappy predecessor? Perhaps, but still usable.

He stared at the noose and considered using it. But not yet, not tonight. Nicky slept and dreamed. Mostly about that champagne.

Next day, Nicky listlessly meandered along the boardwalk. He made several futile visits to the unemployment office where he was reminded more curtly each time, that he was scheduled for three weeks. Finally, with his fourth visit, the office manager, supported by a member of the Point Pleasure police, who looked like a kid who played his back-up on the varsity, banished him until his designated day and time. Nicky feebly attempted to explain that he might not make it that long but his plea fell upon deaf ears.

That night was unseasonably cold and windy at the Underwood. Seeking more suitable shelter, Nicky blindly stumbled until he reached Olympic Sunrise Pier. His family's pier. He recalled many a day and night enjoying its amusements.

He spotted a light glowing out from the center of the pier. The watchman's shack, Nicky remembered; right next to the funhouse. The light glowed, warm and inviting, drawing starving and freezing Nicky toward it like a hapless moth to a flame.

He crawled through a small opening in the chained link fence that blocked access to the pier in the off-season. It was probably the same fence that was there when he was a kid and he and his friends used to sneak in at night. He made his way to the funhouse, hoping not to rouse the watchman. Once inside, he had little trouble finding his way in the dark. It was the same funhouse his father had ordered from Greece years ago. It now seemed quaint and ancient beside the newer flashier rides with their computer driven flashing lights and dizzying speeds and twists and turns.

Nicky remembered the funhouse well enough to recall that if he was sneaky enough, he could find a warm snug place near the center of the funhouse maze, providing the watchman didn't catch him. He used to take girls there to the place where the sphinx recited its riddles. It was silent now, disconnected for the off-season. There would be no vexing questions tonight.

He grinned childishly at how easy it was for him to find his way through the maze after all these years. He stole past a stygian barn that had been set up like a trap allowing no escape until you performed a prodigious feat such as lifting a heavy object or climbing a wall. Nicky had always managed to avoid that part of the maze.

But then he came to the hall of mirrors. The center of the maze was on the other side. Entering, he at once saw himself reflected a hundred different ways. He appeared as he was at various stages of his life. In this mirror, Nicky as star of the high school team; in this one as a little boy bouncing upon the knee of a proud papa. In a third, that same father, now wrathful as Zeus, hurls lightning bolt banishment at his now jaded looking son. As Nicky made his way through the hall of mirrors, he saw a sequence of fading images; himself, as he sank deeper and deeper into dissipation; until finally, staring into the opening of a noose hanging from a rafter in a shadowy place; considering.

As he emerged from the hall of mirrors, he stood face to face with a plaster of Paris statue of Charon, who guarded the gate leading away from the heart of the maze. He wondered why the designer of the funhouse had placed the boatman of Hades as the guide out of the maze. But he was too exhausted to give the matter any thought. He lay down and quickly drifted off to sleep.

He was roused from his sleep by the sound of approaching footsteps. He then saw a solitary beam of lighting bouncing in his direction. The night watchman.

Nicky clutched his overcoat. But it was no magic cape and he could not render himself invisible by draping it over himself. There was no place for him to go. The night was bitter and he was beaten. No one in this world welcomed him or offered him shelter against the indifferent elements that fate had marshaled against him. Gritting his teeth, he held his ground. He could flee no more.

Then he recalled the night watchman, old Mr. Keever. Nicky and his friends would regularly sneak onto the pier and devil the old timer. What fun that was, leading him on merry chases from amusement to amusement; always permitting him to get close enough to think he might catch them but never letting themselves be caught or recognized. Never tired of their sport with old Mr. Keever; running through darkness and laughing; the old man panting; sputtering curses, his narrow beam of light bouncing about wildly dancing in futility.

They marveled at their youth; so swift and inexhaustible; so easily able to outpace and elude their larger, older, wiser pursuer.

Mr. Keever, to his credit in their eyes in this game, never called the police. For him, it became a matter of pride that *he* catch the trespassers.

Nicky giggled as he remembered poor Mr. Keever, impotently showering curses and threats as they ran off down the beach, laughing insolently and shouting promises to return for more fun another night. That giggle was enough to alert the watchman, who now turned toward the center of the maze.

As he passed ever-vigilant Charon, the watchman was knocked down by a slender figure who ran past him in the darkness.

"Won't catch me, Mr. Keever." Nicky squealed, racing out of the funhouse, toward the carousel.

"Hey you, stop!" the puzzled watchman yelled, not knowing what else to say.

He took up the chase as Nicky, taunted, making several prancing circuits 'round the carousel. Eluding the clutches of the other man, Nicky twirled his cap and laughed with childish delight. The guard tossed something at his head and missed. Nicky stuck out his tongue and thumbed his nose playfully. He hadn't felt this good in a long, long time.

"Getting meaner and nastier in your old age, eh Mr. Keever."

"I'll show *you* mean and nasty if I get my hands on you, punk sonnavabitch."

Nicky paused, confused by the unfamiliar edge in the watchman's voice. He looked quickly into his pursuer's face. One old man looks like another. Did it matter after all? One Mr. Keever or another, they're all Mr. Keevers.

Nicky jaunted off toward the Ferris wheel but took a quick detour when he saw that all the chairs had been removed by the maintenance crew and there would be no way for him to do his death defying climb routine. He sped off toward the roller coaster instead.

The climax of any night of playing with Mr. Keever was always the roller coaster chase scene. By the time the old man made the chase up the main summit of the five story high white-washed wooden coaster, he was wheezing so hard, he couldn't even curse or raise his fist to shake at them. They'd leave him up there at the crest of the hill, outlined in moonlight as he bent double to catch his breath and clutching the railing to keep from falling. The look on his face of extreme puzzlement as his tormentors waved up at him from ground level, taunting and laughing, added to his complete humiliation. That look made the kids' night.

"I don't ever want to be that old." Nicky had said more than once, pointing and jeering at the ridiculous old man. And Mr. Keever would stare down at them impotently, his eyes filled with a hatred of youth that the young would never understand.

All of that flashed through Nicky's mind as he now climbed unsteadily up the slope of the roller coaster. The night watchman reappeared in hot pursuit, having stopped at his shack to telephone the police. He hoped to have the pleasure of nabbing this wise-guy himself, but no sense taking chances. He followed Nicky up the track but paused. Nicky was already near the top, urging him on, taunting and laughing.

The roller coaster was located near the very back of the pier. At high tide, now that the beach had shifted with a great deal of it lost to erosion, the ocean rumbled under the pier; sending shockwaves up the slender wooden pillars that anchored the pier in ever-shifting sands. Wave action caused the entire pier to shiver. On a cold, windy night like this, the violence of the sea sent puffs of foam and salt spray up between the planks of the boardwalk where it froze, creating a slick sheet of treacherous ice.

Whether it was the concussion from hitting the ground or the shock of actually falling that killed the watchman is academic. Nicky did not climb down to find out. Still laughing, he finished his climb to the top of the roller coaster. When he did see the man's motionless body lying at the foot of the roller coaster, Nicky did not understand. He happily insisted that he wanted to be chased.

"C'mon Mr. Keever. Wake up and chase me. It's not break time yet. No napping on the job or I'll tell my father." Nicky paused and tried again. "Aw, Mr. Keever, you're no fun anymore. You're old, old man. Never could catch me, Nobody can catch me."

That's how the police found them. Nicky was finally coaxed down by one of the officers, who seemed vaguely familiar. In the meantime, Nicky's father arrived in his capacity as owner of the pier. Lights began flickering on all around the pier.

When the police brought them together, the old man looked into the trespasser's eyes. But when Nicky falteringly tried to meet his gaze, Zeus in the maze suddenly flashed; his lightening bolts blinding the younger man. Nicky looked away. Father seemed to shrink and bend under the unseen weight of a profound sadness. Father and son did not recognize one another or perhaps did but preferred not to acknowledge one another.

The vagabond was led away between two policemen, both of whom Nicky recalled from high school.

"Hey guys, maybe we can stop for a bottle of wine and sneak into the dance over at rec." He said as they led him past the funhouse.

"Rogue Wave"

He remembered the first time he tried to body surf, when he was a little kid. He was so excited when he caught the wave that he forgot to close his mouth. He swallowed enough water and other marine flotsam to fill a respectable salt water aquarium. If he'd been a whale with a throat full of baleen, he could have gulped down a decent afternoon snack. Instead, he nearly drowned. But he did learn the first rule about bodysurfing: always keep your mouth shut when you hit the waves and you'll never wind up with a mush full of mullet.

He learned something about his mother that day, too. She scolded him after he'd been hauled out of the water, choking and gagging himself blue in the face. She wasn't upset about his brush with death. He'd embarrassed her in front of "all those week-enders". She had never felt comfortable sharing the beach with them. The beach was directly in front of her huge "summer cottage", a massive marble mansion her husband had had built as a monument to his affluence. She considered that beach to be her private property. She'd been embarrassed by the lack of dignity he'd displayed as the result of his lack of oxygen.

She never went in the water herself and, hence, had no clue as to what it was like to swallow half an ocean.

The father, as usual, was off somewhere earning the piles of money needed to keep his family comfortably sequestered. His father had no idea about the lives he was underwriting. He was content not knowing, so long as he could maintain them at a comfortable distance.

The boy learned that common sense determined the golden rule governing this personal sport of his. Common sense and survival became his mantras since there were no teachers or coaches or role models he could turn to. He counted on the ocean to teach him and it did so, with its inexhaustible supply of waves and endless variations on the savage elements theme.

After he learned that he had to keep his mouth shut, he learned that he should never body surf when there is lightning on the ocean. This maxim he discovered in all its grisly detail, the day he witnessed a man on a surf board get zapped. By the time the surfer washed up on the beach, he had been reduced to a blackened cinder. His once shiny fiberglass surf board had been vaporized.

The wrath of God. The unleashed fury of the naked elements. Call it how you saw it. That wave spit that surfer onto the beach and then faded away with the same indifference its fellows had shown a zillion less eventful times that day.

In youthful contests with his older brother, his mother safely removed on her marble balcony where she swilled gin and tonics and tuned them out, the idea was to see who could ride the farthest. They would pick out targets; cute girls, old ladies. The brother would cheat and scramble along the bottom using his hands to scuttle along. But he was always honest with the wave. Even then, as a kid, he felt the anticipation for the next wave; that it would be bigger, its curl more supple, the ride lasting longer. Always something better to anticipate; a longer ride; the endless opportunism of optimism.

The brother gave up on it, young, and took to surf boards; then jet skis; then cigarette boats before finally leaving the ocean altogether. Corresponding to that sequence of events, the brother went off to college, found a job and met a girl who was just right but turned out to be otherwise and, finally having cut off all contact with unresponsive parents, moved away. But he persisted in seeking the rogue wave.

He had never taken to the idea of riding on boards. Even as a youngster, while his brother and friends were caught up in the social mystique of the surfing craze, he remained a firm, mystical believer in dealing with water which he felt to be the particular element guiding his destiny, on its own terms and unaided by man-made devices of any kind. Simply put, he liked to keep both feet on the ground; an essential starting point from which the bodysurfer gets a good push into an onrushing wave.

Swim out to the sandbar. Three, four effortless strokes that inflates him with a feeling of power. He hopes the girls are watching. Now wait and build up that reserve of energy needed for the ride. The water is crowded but he is always alone when he bodysurfs. Just him and the wave. Never him *versus* the ocean. Sandbars are ideal launching pads for body surfers. The sandbar liberates the bodysurfer from lingering in the wading area dodging the kids, the old timers, the timid.

Over the years, since nearly swallowing that first wave, bodysurfing had become a form of traveling to him. Like walking. His mother had long since stopped coming to the beach with him; choosing instead to retreat to the isolated comfort of her beachfront balcony where she could look down on everything and scowl.

From the moment he rode that first wave, he'd embarked upon a quest for bigger and better waves. The quest shaped him. He evolved into a sun-wizened beach bum; stoically squinting at oncoming waves, ever-assessing and anticipating, ever looking over the shoulder of the approaching wave at the one following and so forth, always in search of the perfect wave.

What is the *perfect* wave? He was uninterested in what the California beach boys had to say on the subject. He'd read about their contests where riders wearing numbers cavorted in bodysurfing outfits complete with caps and fins to allow them to shear through the water with less resistance. It all lacked purity. He wasn't interested in competing with people. His was a holy quest to find and master the perfect wave.

He knew what the concept meant to him.

The perfect wave would carry him effortlessly, without twisting or pounding his torso, without filling his trunks with a dune's worth of sand. The perfect wave would propel him swiftly to the beach and only the land would stop him from continuing forever. When he was a teenager, he included the admiring bikini-clad blonde as an integral part of the perfect wave.

"Can you show me how to do that?" she asks.

"That, and so much more." He answers, cryptically in that adolescent scene played out in those younger fantasies.

He was older now, no longer slathered in suntan lotion, no longer flopped on the blanket all day between riding sessions, nonchalantly working on just the right tan. The opulence of time to squander was gone. His forehead wrinkled. He had to wear hats now. The body he'd once been so proud of now bore scars and showed the paunchy ravages of time spent tarrying.

And while he still had an eye for the ladies, he didn't perform feats in the water for their entertainment anymore. The bikini clad babes fade into one another in memory. These days, it was himself and the wave and the primordial force welding them together.

The sheer enormity and indifference of the sea drew him to it. The way it roared and crashed one minute, while gently lapping at the edge of the land the next. The way it casually tossed onto the beach, millions of dead creatures of endless variety to horrify and amaze beach walkers. There was the other thing too; the feeling thing. The way his contact with the sea made him feel less bitter, washing away hard feelings toward people in macrocosm and his parents, in microcosm, etcetera.

Having lived his entire life essentially alone, the sea his companion; he was cooled and soothed by his countless hours riding the waves. And while he still had the physical needs of a land-based creature for his elements: air to breath, water to drink, food to eat, pleasure to distract him; these were reduced to secondary importance to his pursuit of the wave.

One summer, in a pique of anger caused by his having rattled his mother once too often, she had exiled him from the family bosom; from its marble mansion, and its bank accounts. He was forced to live by his wits and negotiate a living from the local tourism industry.

While he lived that particular summer largely hand to mouth, his was still an idyllic existence; strumming an undersized guitar as he swung in a hammock hung between two clearly out of place and dying palm trees planted near the beach by Point Pleasure's crackerjack Public Works crew. The trees were the delight of tourists who stood in line to pose for photographs for $6 a pop; swinging in that hammock wearing a straw boater pink soft drink concoction in one hand, parasol in the other with a fake blue sea and sky cardboard background so that the photographer could guarantee that the elements were always cooperative for photos snapped at this resort.

Forced to sell out; he had taken this job as "colorful local character", creating picture postcards with simpleton captions like "wish you were here" that tourists could bring back to their one horse town existences and regale the locals with tales of times spent "in the islands".

For an extra buck, he'd not only snap the pictures; he'd pose for one or two; his colorful local character costume consisting of palm frond hat and four day beard and decadently bleary-eyed countenance from too many margaritas swilled in the back seat of his '69 Mustang convertible that didn't run but sat parked, prop-like, next to his concession.

He needed the money. His heart wasn't in the work. The smiles he flashed for every Hazel and Burt from Dubuque were as fake as that perpetually blue cardboard sky he served up to the paying customers.

His true grin reappeared at workday's end when he hit the waves. He would squint and fix upon the horizon, waiting for that one rogue wave that comes along once in a lifetime and catching that wave would finally erase all the scorn and bitterly amused contempt he felt for himself and the world and every tacky man jack in it. He'd lift a whelk and instead of blowing sea notes into it, he would hold it to his ear and listen, hoping to catch a murmur of the rogue but instead hearing only his mother's harpy voice or the buffoonish cackles of the rubes lining up to be taken.

The need to work inconvenienced him for one summer. His mother took him back come September and his day job experience faded into unpleasant memory.

He used to imagine himself being watched by judges on the beach, aloof figures who resembled his parents They were raised above the gathered crowds and sat perched in the clouds watching and judging every nuance of every move he made within the waves. Evaluating the quality of his ride. All eyes fall upon him as he treaded water and watched and waited for the right wave. All the others would overanxiously try the lesser waves and come up short, either missing the ride altogether or falling short of the beach.

Then, the right wave would come and he would nonchalantly ride it to the beach. The judges muttered but showed no sign. Admiring eyes of the crowd upon him.

Sometimes, you have to work more, swim faster and push harder to catch the wave. The true bodysurfer knows his beach, the slope of the tidal plain, the dynamics of the waves as they cross the shelf before finally cresting and making for their ultimate demise at the water's end. A good bodysurfer can float or stand and be in perfect position to catch any wave.

In the belly of the wave you are in its control. And yet, *you* control. Using all your skill and experience to meld with it and harmonize with its motions. The wave can discard the rider easily and does so indifferently.

The ride requires perfect timing. Head out just in front of the foaming, crashing crest of the wave. Remembering that these are the same waves that eat entire sections of beach in quick ferocious gulps, the rider knows what it could do to him. But it is in the front of the wave that the ride is best; where the wave action is most powerful and movement the swiftest.

Plunging shoreward, arms extended as in flight, body taut and hard as a board yet pliable enough to move with the inner movements of the wave even as it begins to break and crashes and powers him forward on its surge. Eyes open to watch the beach and himself in the context of the ride.

One day, in a later summer, still capable of enjoying such lighthearted fantasy, he created an entire competition, sponsored by his favorite beer company. Open to all, but the best riders were men like himself, aged past their primes, physiques given to paunch from drinking their sponsor's product. The down time between rides passes in good natured ribbing about the rides being shorter because of beer bellies dragging along the bottom and waves being missed because winded geezers couldn't get back out fast enough to catch them. But there was the camaraderie of frequent beer breaks.

A good body surfer not only knows the waves and tides, he knows the moon and her moods and phases. A good body surfer has a sense of timing. He knows to hit the waves after a storm has subsided but not necessarily fully blown out to sea. On such a day, breeze out of the north, cool and dry. Wind straight off the beach from behind the dunes. A full moon. And there as if by magic, a sand bar appears about a hundred yards out. Because of the way the wind is blowing, the waves come on forming cylinders. Spray delicately flickers off the crest of each as they barrel shoreward at seemingly perfect intervals. The water is clear. He can see his toes. To anyone who has watched waves in action, they seem to come in sets of three. On such a day, each wave is a rider; the third usually best, crest to base about seven feet. He noted that the water and air temperatures were roughly identical which meant you could stay in and ride for hours, which he does. He had to be there now. Next day, he knew from experience, the sand bar would be gone and it would be different.

Looking out from the cylinders, he searched in vain for the rogue but instead, saw only those frowning judges, watching closely; never pleased until he finally lassoed and conquered the rogue.

The next day *was* different. The ocean was angry. It raged to swallow the beach, chewing chunks of sand, hoping to get at the people in the hotels and the gaudy mansions behind the dune line. On such days, the waves rush uncaring right to the edge of the sea and fling themselves with all their might at the land; scattering billions of granules of sand into the water. On these days, rip tides twist the bodysurfer indifferently, his ears and nose and trunks clogged with sand, his teeth will still grind for days after such an encounter.

Point Pleasure Crest was an enclave of affluence at the northern tip of the barrier island that contained the much larger, more famous tourist town of Point Pleasure. The Crest remained his home base over the years, even during those emotional lean times when mother shooed him away and father was what he always had been, a nonpresence.

He had never felt at home in the stately marble manor that served as his residence. It didn't seem inconsistent to him that his father, whose own road to fortune had started as a developer of the gaudy resort to the south, now distanced himself as much as possible from that place. Afterall, he had the same attitude toward his wife and sons.

The waves had always been better at the northern tip of the island so he didn't follow in his brother's footsteps and make tracks out of there to set up on his own at the first reasonable opportunity. Given that taking tourist pictures was his only attempt at participating in the world of work, his skills in practical matters of survival were severely lacking.

He'd grown up in boarding schools so as not to be tainted by the plebian values of local public schools. That had been his mother's idea. She was unrelenting in her efforts to maintain her son's social aloofness. It had been mother who had been at least physically present in his youthful moments of sickness and doubt; though her emotional distance awed him with her terrible power and taught him to stand defiantly alone.

She believed in the power of the will. Her will. She had willed herself out of a life of seediness in Point Pleasure, "that town down the road" where she'd been born and lived until she had coerced a husband into building this isolated castle in the sand with polished stone imported from old world quarries; ostentatiously plopping it down at the northern end.

She had willed herself into fixed prosperity even when that husband for all intents and purposes abandoned her to pursue a separate life.

As soon as he was old enough to gracefully do so, he left his mother's smothering custody. But he never completely broke away. There was still the matter of the monthly allowance check, always right on time and firmly in hand. So armed, he set out to explore the rest of the world; a world that she had promised him he would find dreary.

She was right to an extent. Land and its dominant species, he did find dreary. But wherever he traveled, he was drawn to beaches and to the wave action of those beaches. Each summer, he returned to the family home.

Though he traveled far and kept careful watch for the elusive rogue wave and had immersed himself in each of the world's great seas, he could find no waves anywhere to compare with those at Point Pleasure Crest. Once, when he mentioned the rogue wave to his mother she sniffed and noted that it would be poetic justice for such a wave to strike "just down the road" and wash away that "blight of carnival nightmares that your father, has given to the world". He had always imagined the rogue striking his island home and wiping clean a lot of slates.

Events always carried him back to his place of origin. On one visit home, he learned that his father had died. The sea roared but the waves were pedestrian. The rogue did not appear that day.

On a later occasion he had come home to announce that he had "nearly married". The sea rose abnormally high and the waves chewed up a hundred yards of beachfront before subsiding. About the same time as his ardor to enter the state of matrimony. And then, the sea was calm.

Home again now at the start of another summer, he found his invincible mother in her sick bed. The earth trembled and the sea was mass of churning foam.

"Stay with me to the end." She demanded before changing her tone and asking him pitiably.

He went to the beach that afternoon while she slept fitfully.

"I have never been so close to being required to confront my own mortality." He thought as he waited on a wave that had risen about thirty yards out from where he tread water. Death raced through his mind as his body hurtled shoreward.

His mother's deterioration had disturbed him more than he'd ever imagined it would. She had been imperturbable strength, the rock upon which all the wild waters of his life had broken without apparent effect. While he had avoided her, neglected her, pretended she wasn't there; she had always been there waiting, taming tempests by the strength of her will. Now as she faded, would the rogue come?

Suddenly, fog crossed ahead of him, moving quickly landward. The fog enveloped him before he could get out of the water. It was thick and he could no longer see the beach or the horizon in the other direction. He felt truly alone inside a bubble of fog.

He swam toward the sand bar when he heard loud splashing to his right. Dolphins, six or seven, moved his way. Dodging and riding the waves with an effortless skill that he both admired and envied, they approached within several yards of where he tread water.

The dolphins were huge, about eight to ten feet in length, all sleek and glistening muscle. He marveled at a youngster about half that size and how it stayed at its mother's side as they all played and swam, breathed and dived.

Dolphins swam beneath him and leaped over him. He reached up and gently stroked a smooth belly. Perfect shape, perfect symmetry, perfect skin for bodysurfing, he mused. As if reading his mind, the dolphins began riding, They rode simply for the joy of it. Schools of fish swam past unmolested. The dolphins were having too much fun to think of food.

Suddenly, another shape entered through the fog; a shark. The dolphins worked together to fend off the shark. Again and again, the shark attacked, trying to get at the youngster. The dolphins parried, confronting those razor sharp teeth while protecting the young one with their bodies.

When the shark turned its attention on him, the dolphins surrounded him and protected him the same way. The shark finally got the message and swam off to lick its wounds.

All that work made the dolphins hungry. They began to feed on the passing fish with the same vigor they'd shown in play and combat. Fascinated, he watched as they toyed with their catch and feasted. Several times, it seemed to him that the dolphins were inviting him to join their close-knit family but he kept a distance, satisfied with watching.

A rising full moon penetrated the fog. He rejoined the dolphins near the sand bar. He used this to launch himself; catching several waves while the dolphins playfully teased a blue claw crab unlucky enough to be crossing the bar.

Moonlight glistened off the dolphins' backs scattering millions of fragments of golden light across the water as he and the dolphins bodysurfed late into the night. The fog finally lifted, revealing a star-filled sky. The dolphins headed out to open sea.

He was surprised to find that he had been quite close to the beach and within view of his mother's balcony, the entire time. He looked up at the house in time to see a frail shadow that had been standing at the window, outlined in a dim light.

He left that night, without bidding his mother farewell; to seek the rogue wave, searching through receding wisps of fog.

He wasn't proud of much. There was his year round tan, acquired at considerable expense in time and his family's money. Other than that brief summer stint as beach photographer/colorful local character, he'd never held a job. A monthly stipend, sustained him as he wandered the globe, a child who never grew up but continued into adulthood and middle age still a child.

He gave no thought to settling down and raising a family of his own. Having considered the prospect and what the arrangement had done to his peers, he avoided commitment with the same energy he used to elude stinging jellyfish that frequently crossed his path in the water. There had been women, lots of them; or at least enough of them to give him something to think about when he lay in the sun with nothing else to occupy his thoughts but to recoup his strength for his next attempt to locate and ride the rogue.

He had always felt trapped and squeamish when he spoke to his mother, whether in person during a visit or on the phone. And while he always felt a bit of shyness, a hesitation when he opened her elegant letters and found the check; there was a stirring of what might have been guilt in someone else but for him it was little more than a realization that something wasn't right. Was the check her way of maintaining tenuous control or an uncomfortable parent's awkward way of expressing love? He always managed to overcome nagging scruples in time to make it to the drive-through teller's before the window closed.

He'd wanted to be at his mother's side when she died but, instead, found himself on a beach in Hawaii, enjoying one of those textbook perfect bodysurfing days. He'd have been back for the funeral but one day ran into another and he couldn't drag himself away. He knew that his mother would never have understood.

She had hated the beach despite living out most of her life within view of it. She had always feared the sea, an element in her life that was too big and wild for her to exercise her will over. In her last loneliest years, she would sit for hours on her marble balcony watching the sea and cursing it; hoping that it might finally rise up and come for her and carry her away to its cold dark vastness.

Her death, when it finally came, had been painless. There had been no deathbed dramatics. She had died alone in the night and the sea had been calm.

That, somehow, comforted him and eased any feeling of guilt.

The Point Pleasure Crest house was worth several million dollars, or so decreed the real estate vultures, who hovered about him when he came back for the last time. His older brother would never return to this country, having established a life for himself as an investment banker in Amsterdam. He had no use for the rambling marble monolith and wanted done with the mundane chore of disposing of it. The brother had left the entire matter in his hands, suggesting only that he'd best talk to a lawyer he recommended from Philadelphia, an old college friend.

"You may know all about waves but you don't know a thing about sharks in three piece suits." They shared a long distance laugh. They signed off with almost sincere guarantees that they'd get together sometime that year. "In Portgugal, perhaps."

The morning he finally settled the matter of the house, he sat on the beach just under that balcony. It was a typical beach day, sun shining, gulls stealing French fries out of the hands of children; volleyballs bouncing into the dunes.

Ice cream vendors hawk their fudgy wudgies. Youngsters build sand castles at the water's edge and scream in frustration when the ocean rolls over and washes them away and the kids run crying to the parents and the parents, trying to relax and get a few minutes peace, send them back to build another. Teenagers cuddle on a blanket nearby. Like always...to facilitate rites of passage are the reason beaches and the sea were created. For others.

Into the midst of this picture postcard summer afternoon, the rogue wave rises up.

Having traveled across the Atlantic from the Canary Islands it had remained hidden in summery haze so thick that it can approach rushing upon the unsuspecting beach. Just as it crosses the horizon, picking up speed and water for its frontal assault, the fog dissipates, revealing the rogue in all its uncaring power and white-capped majesty.

Life guards see it first and don't know what to do. There is no signal they can use to communicate the fact that this one hundred foot high monster is heading their way and there is no way to get 100,000 people off the beach.

Ineffectually, they whistle everyone out of the water as the wave rolls over cigarette boats and jet skis and fishing boats as it rolls shoreward getting still bigger. It's a true rogue, defying all the laws of physics, geology, and all the other sciences.

People stand stupidly at the water's edge and watch. Then, *he* steps forward.

He strides purposefully out and dives and starts swimming toward the wave. He catches it just as it begins to curl and white froth is everywhere as the very guts and sinew and soul of the sea strain inside this wave. The ocean is mustering one great effort to retake the land and establish its watery dominion over all the pathetic rabble now gathered awe-struck in the path of the rogue.

He rides the curl like Pecos Bill lassoing the tornado. Hands extended out of the curl, he waves to the crowd, recalling those Marvel *Submariner* comic book pastels and the entire scene dissolves into a speeded-up cartoon. Everyone runs piggledly-wiggledly into each other slapstick fashion all squealing like Alvin and the Chipmunks. He can't explain why all of a sudden this comic book imagery comes to mind. The crowd is frozen there on the beach, a hundred feet beneath him and the onrushing water. The wave rushes across the beach scattering people like ants before indifferently swallowing them up.

Dunes vanish and the wave doesn't stop. The bulkhead is reduced to splinters and the water rushes forward. Still he's riding near the summit of the wave and whooping now; yahooing with his arms extended out front as the wave tears into the boardwalk and sends the Ferris wheel spinning westward, a whirling hoop; next stop Nebraska.

The rogue is insatiable, gobbling up priceless real estate as it heads across Point Pleasure island offering him a spectacular view of the non-discriminating devastation. South at Point Pleasure; motels, hotels, condos, townhouses, boarding houses, bungalows and trailers; cars, trucks, vans, humvees, SUV's, motorcycles, satellite television dishes, screen porches, ice cream stands, pizza joints, restaurants, bars, taverns, Irish pubs, nightclubs, miniature golf courses, tee shirt joints, tattoo parlors, piercing parlors, beauty salons, rigged boardwalk game wheels, Point Pleasure City Hall, and the entire boardwalk, the while damn mess purged from the land and swept clean by the rogue.

Once the wave broke, there would be one helluva let down and one helluva mess and one helluva challenge to make something meaningful out of the mess.

The ride lasted a lifetime and was over in a heartbeat.

Picking seaweed out of his toes and grinding the sand in his teeth. His shoulders ached from steering his way through the rogue which finally veered back to the north and demolished all the mansions of the wealthy at Point Pleasure Crest. All but one squatting marble monolith. The wave finally deposited him on his mother's balcony. He pulled himself to his feet unsteadily and looked over the railing. Looking out, he saw that all on the island had perished. Except himself. Everything on the island had been destroyed and washed away. The last thing he saw before blacking out was a pellucid hand, an old woman's hand, reaching out to him. But unable to make contact.

He woke up wondering about his dream. Was his rogue wave really a pillar of salt sent by a wrathful God to smite the sinful and wasteful greed and harlotry of Point Pleasure? And the frothing white foam in the teeth of the wave assumed the shapes of avenging angels wielding swords of watery flame…

And who was *he*, riding the wave through and over that cleansing, a lost soul floating? And who belonged to the hand? He had trouble imagining his mother assuming the role of angel, dream or no dream.

Nice thing about salt water. Allows for plenty of buoyancy, not a bad quality When all you want to do is just go with the flow. He suddenly started thinking about Thailand. Great waves there.

He quickly arranged to sell the house to a writer he had gotten to know from afternoons of body surfing and beer drinking. Together, they had beerily concocted a scheme to make body surfing an Olympics event open only to middle-aged men with a suitably developed paunch. Cold beer flowing at every training session.

The writer had visited the mansion to use the outside shower after one particularly sandy session in the waves. He'd been impressed with its many decks and how each deck offered a unique and scenic view of the sea, the island, and the back bay area. He'd been amused by the incongruity of the marble; so unsuited to a sand bar but yet so fitting a statement of American affluence and waste. He'd dedicate it as a cathedral to his quest to recall simplicity and balance…

Still, all in all, it was a bit of prime real estate; last standing structure on an otherwise devastated island at the Jersey shore.

The writer had walked away from a stressful post, editing a major urban newspaper. He was embarking upon a new career, book contract in hand, as a bodysurfer in print pursuing truth, justice, and the lost way.

Knowing the brother in Amsterdam wouldn't mind, he'd given the writer a large discount on the asking price much to the chagrin of the realtors who wept and took out their calculators and refigured their six percent

"This writer's a pretty good body surfer." He explained to the telephone. "Besides, he offered me an easement. I can crash here anytime I come through looking for waves."

He could focus wholly on Thailand now; where the waves are perpetually perfect and there were women. A middle-aged bodysurfer with a pocket full of the local currency need not entertain any more questions about his purpose in life.

"Rewritten Endings"

My old man was a young man when he died. Cancer. Too many cigarettes. Too much time spent in city traffic, inhaling exhaust fumes and suppressing anger. Too many years in factories and poorly ventilated warehouses, doing things he hated doing; always dreaming of escaping with his fishing rod to a nice quiet place on the beach. Too much boiling rage at his station in life. Too much planning for a future that just never seemed to be getting any closer to happening.

His helplessness to alter the course of events that guided him from day to day had left a dark blotch on his spirit. The blotch grew and grew every day, week, year. Until the cancer killed him. Way before his time, actuarially speaking; yet years after life had ceased to offer him anything but frustration and a dwindled hope for achieving an acceptable compromise.

It had been a mercy that he went when he did. A mercy to him. A mercy to my mother, who was his devoted caregiver all through the radiation, the chemo, and then more radiation and more chemo. The doctors were ready to prolong his ordeal; as they had for the better part of three years. But what was the point? He didn't want to continue. He'd been reduced to a state of helpless infancy; his mind gone except for one corner where he kept his rage. *That* part remained crystal clear and active to the very end.

I wasn't there when he died. I was at the Jersey shore, at the family summer place in Point Pleasure. That's ironic because I didn't really want to be at the shore but a series of circumstances landed me there. Ironic because the shore is the place where he would have chosen to go to die. I know that because it's the place where he'd always wanted to live.

Even in the act of dying, he'd been helpless to control his own affairs. The last time I saw him, he was shriveled up and hairless. He looked like a freakish infant. He had the newborn's blindness. He could not speak and could barely hear. He needed help to get out of the bed to go to the bathroom and had to be watched even there; which humiliated him. Humiliation was one of the few feelings he was permitted to feel besides the rage.

I wanted to kill him during my last visit. He wanted me to kill him. He asked me to do so, out of mercy if not out of love. As with most of the important moments of truth in my life up to now, I flubbed it. Couldn't bring myself to do it. Instead, I retreated and hid behind the nurse. I told her he was speaking out of his head. She medicated him and he slept. In the end, I had betrayed him. I knew that the moment he asked me to kill him that his mind was as clear and sharp as it had ever been. Once again, he was trying to exercise his will over his fate. It was not his to control.

I know now, as I approach the middle of my own life, what I should have done.

I should have lifted all eighty-nine pounds of him out of the bed, with his tubes and blankets and bedpans and bottles of painkillers. I should have lifted him the way Jesus raised Lazarus from the ignominy of his deathbed. I should have pushed past the protesting nurse and the sobbing relatives. I should have taken him out of that house and away from that grey killing city.

I should have brought him to the Jersey shore.

Years after his funeral, I met the old man one night. He walked into the grand re-opening of the new Buddy's Bar in Point Pleasure and asked me to buy him a beer. He wasn't carrying any money seeing as he no longer needed it at his new location. Under ordinary circumstances, he would have plunked a $20 bill on the bar and ordered his own drink. He'd always insisted on paying his own way.

I'd been at the bar most of the afternoon and was actually just getting ready to leave when he showed up. My friends had all headed off to their respective homes and families, making an early night of even such an auspicious occasion as the reopening of our old "hang out" under new ownership.

I did a double take when I saw him, but since so many old Buddy's regulars had shown up for the re-opening, including a few we had been sure were dead, his appearance at his favorite bar in Point Pleasure didn't come as such a shock

I glanced at his shoulders, expecting to see angel wings or some sort of insignia of his new status. No wings, no haloes; not even a Boy Scout merit badge. So I checked the top of his head for horns and looked behind him to see if he was dragging a long pointy tail; badges of another, hotter destination.

"Where have they gone and put you, dad?" I asked, not seeing any sort of identifying accoutrements. "They didn't reopen Limbo just for you, did they?"

He laughed at my attempt at sacrilegious humor but offered no answer; being intent upon watching the artistry of the bar tender who was pouring beers into frosted mugs.

"Buddy's use frosted mugs now?" he asked with a disdainful shake of the head.

"It's a fern bar now, dad." I answered.

The bartender brought dad's beer in the silver stein he'd been buried with. I'd brought it home for him from one of my youthful trips to Ireland. I'd had his name engraved on it, along with something in Gaelic that I can't remember now. He drank deep before pausing to look around. He shuddered, a bit uncomfortable at the idea of being in Point Pleasure on a work night, in the off-season.

I waited to hear what he had to say but he didn't talk. Too busy looking around; taking in the atmosphere of the bar. I could tell by the evident pleasure showing in his eyes, that he was enjoying this new found leisure of his. He suggested that he would meet me at Buddy's the next morning so we could rent a boat and go out for some flounder fishing over in Hereford's Inlet.

I ordered another round and reminded him that I had to work. He winced softly at that, the idea of me going to work. He suggested I play hooky. It was my turn to laugh. So far as I know, he had never "played hooky" from work a day in his life; had never called out sick either; at least, not until the cancer set in for keeps. I told him that my days of carefree wantonness were over. He shook his head knowingly and softly told me that I should always make room for play. After that, we stood side by side at the bar, quietly drinking. I wondered at his change of heart toward my approach to work.

"Even with eternity, time is precious. There's so much going on and everything interests me now." He shrugged. "I use time to do whatever I feel like doing."

He went back to his beer.

I want to re-write my father's ending. Instead of being my usual peripheral, ineffectual character, I assume a hero's role in my father's revised death scene.

It begins with me staunchly standing up to the medical staff and relatives who tell me that the old man shouldn't be moved because it wouldn't be good for him. I say nothing. I simply gesture at the old man, drooling uncontrollably as he slumps in his wheel chair while I battle the meddlesome do-gooders.

No need for me to say a word with that vivid image.

How, that image begs, could he *possibly* be worse?

The medical people insist upon practicing their mumbojumbo. But at least the relatives get a clue and see the logic of what I'm showing them.

They take the fight to the paid professionals while I take up my paternal bundle and sneak out the back door.

I race down the street to my car as city-imprisoned neighbors, curious about the hullabaloo coming from the sick house, tear themselves away from their boob tubes long enough to come out on their porches. Seeing me toting the old man, tubes and wires popping and fizzling and dangling all around him, with clear intentions of breaking out of there and making for healthier, wider, opener spaces; the neighbors let up a collective banshee wail and beg me to take them along.

I lie to these zombies and promise I'll come back for them, kicking them off as they clutch my feet in supplication. The old man rolls his good eye and gleefully curses at them as we make good our escape.

We beat the toll at the bridge, zipping through Easy Pass at an easy 95 miles per. "Been wanting to do that for years!" the old man wheezes, already winning the struggle to regain control of himself. And we're off across southern New Jersey.

There's a high speed chase down the Atlantic City Expressway far more dramatic than the nationally televised scene with OJ's white Bronco. Local, county, and state cops are after us in cruisers and vans. There are even a couple of helicopters dogging me all the way to the turnoff exit for the Garden State Parkway, onto which we head south toward Point Pleasure.

Tourist filled family vans pull over to gawk and casino excursion buses filled with 'white heads' bound for the slot machines of Atlantic City honk, the drivers cheering me on and helping with impromptu road blocks thrown up to disrupt the pursuit. The sky overhead fills with Action News choppers from New York and Philly. These interfere with the police helicopters, and the overcrowded sky results in several spectacular aerial collisions and explosions. The flatlands and marshes of southern New Jersey are littered with television equipment and bits and pieces of splattered media personalities.

All the while, me and the old man are splitting a gut from laughing at the entire madcap adventure all the way down to near the end of the Cape May peninsula when we make the turn and head east, seaward toward Point Pleasure.

Our first stop, once we drive onto the island, is Buddy's Bar. Not that we needed a drink, although the thought did cross both our minds. Stopping at Buddy's first before going to our summer place, was something of a family tradition going back to the earliest years that our family had the place at Point Pleasure. The old man and I used to drive down every Saturday morning in the off-season to work on fixing up the old dump he'd bought while rendered temporarily insanely adventuresome, under control of his escape dream. In those days, the place had no heat and the old man always shut off the water in mid October. So after a two hour drive, and fortified with the knowledge that home was not the place to go, we discovered that Buddy's made an ideal pit stop.

Over the years, as we got to know Point Pleasure and I became old enough to partake of refreshment a little stronger than cola and "slim jim", our visits to Buddy's became more frequent and lasted longer with each trip to the shore.

Buddy's was a locals place. Tourists avoided it for the same reasons that locals loved it. The ladies' rest room was usually out of order. It was perpetually dark inside the bar, like the womb and the tomb. Buddy's always stank of stale beer and urine and no one could determine which was which. And Buddy's proudly never served a drink garnished with a colorful plastic umbrella.

The floor at Buddy's had a decided slant, skewing reality all the more for its befuddled patrons by leading them with the force of gravity directly toward the heart of the bar, its inner sanctum. Here, local wags, pundits, and practical jokers held court daily. Anyone hoping to obtain a libation at Buddy's had to pass under the intense and usually critical scrutiny of this impressive crew of hangabouts, loafers, and desperadoes.

My father came to know them all on a first name basis and considered it to be the apex of social achievement to be genuinely greeted whenever he happened into the place.

My father could recite the history of his chosen haunt with more thoroughness and enthusiasm than he brought to most of the other activities of his daily life.

He told me that Buddy's had once been the home of the Point Pleasure Volunteer Fire Company. There was a yellowed photograph behind the bar of a bunch of rough looking rustic types huddled around a horse and what looked like a huge spittoon on wheels. This, I learned, was the original Point Pleasure Volunteer Fire Company with their equipment.

On either side of that photo, were autographed black and white glossies of Philadelphia Phillies Whiz Kid Richie Ashburn and New York Yankees pitcher Whitey Ford. Both before my time but contemporaries of the old man and the regulars. Legend has it that, at one time or other, both of these bigger than life characters, bent an elbow at Buddy's. These photographs constituted the sum total of the décor for the bar.

The firehouse had been converted into a saloon after the war (Second). The last vestiges of Prohibition had blown seaward and Buddy, the Olympian figure who gave the bar its name, came out of the neighborhoods of South Philadelphia and invested himself in full splendor behind the taps of his very own saloon at the shore.

The old man's eyes would literally mist over when he recalled that event. Buddy had been a personal hero for him; a man who had made the break and come out a winner.

It had been a part of the old man's retirement dream to become one of the regulars at Buddy's. Any graduate student in "litterchore" seeking to find that literary quality known as "local color" is advised to put in a few hours bending an ear and an elbow at Buddy's in the course of doing the doctoral dissertation.

At any given hour, on any given day, one would encounter Muldoon, a retired bachelor Chemistry teacher of 34 years from Point Pleasure Public High School. Muldoon's daily tirades against the slings and arrows of adolescent female hormones, interspersed with snippets from show tunes and bawdy bits of vaudeville and medievalia sung in husky baritone, were sheer music and poetry for the tired ears of the barfly.

Muldoon was also master of the never ending story. As much of the history of Point Pleasure is actually a recitation of the lifelines of the town's many bars, anyone hoping to hold the floor at Buddy's had better know where he's been drinking. Muldoon is holding forth the night the old man and I escape to Buddy's. As we slide down closer to catch a bit of what he said, Muldoon doesn't miss a beat or come up for air.

"So I went over to Five Minute Dave's for a trim." Muldoon explains to no one in particular. "I call him *Five* Minute Dave even though I know the rest of you have always called him Two Minute Dave but he's gotten older and a bit slow so I added a few minutes to his name. Not that it matters with my sparsity of hair since it only took him a minute and a half. Not even long enough for him to tell me about the new owners of Liam's Pub next door."

"I wonder if they're going to change the name again. Seems like just last summer that it was McAteer's Irish Saloon and Jewish Deli. I guess the rye didn't mix with the rye, so to speak, heh heh." He pauses for a sip of beer and croons a few lines from a Sina-tra song. The bar man raises a threatening eye brow, nods at a sign that expressly forbids singing in church. Muldoon stops in mid-phrase.

"And before McAteer had it, it was Kelso's. The same Kelso as had it in Port Richmond where they used to serve the ten cent beers all day Sundays and they had the pool tables."

All the while, the old man nods. Remembering the afternoons *he'd* slipped out, ostensibly for a quick trim at Two Minute Dave's but really for a two beer stop at McAteer's or Kelso's or...

"Crawford's Café. That was back in the Sixties. The Crawford brothers took turns tending bars. They were the singing school teachers. Mark Crawford used to run the beach patrol back then. Got my nephew on when he was pretending to work his way through college only he was working his way through every waitress on the island."

Dad laughs. We have all forgotten the original point of Muldoon's discourse, knowing that there really is no point.

But it doesn't matter. The recitation of the lineage of that particular bar has, intended or otherwise, evoked several streams of memories. It is a local cultural fact that the common thread of the tap room link my father and Muldoon and all the others around the bar; people who otherwise have nothing in common. As Muldoon burst into song.

The other regulars comprise something of a cross section, representative of that famed yet never found American melting pot. There's Harmon, a Gulf War vet, who routinely bemoaned his fate in arriving at a still young age; to a state of being married with four strapping youngsters and him driving a delivery truck for a local beer distributor.

Or Calloway, the resoundingly unsuccessful "great white hope" heavyweight boxer who slumped over the bar at almost seven feet tall, possessing the grace of a toddler. Calloway is big with the regulars who thought he was tough but quickly learned that he is also dumb. To the point that Calloway is often the unwitting butt of their witticisms. But they also look up to him because Calloway had parlayed his unsuccessful boxing career into a modestly successful movie career and in his drunker moments, he speaks dreamily of bringing a film crew to Point Pleasure and to Buddy's Bar. His presence adds cosmopolitan overtones to the place. One expected television interviewers, groupies, movie producer-types, and autograph hounds to swarm all over Buddy's any time Calloway stopped in for a couple of beers.

That was some your year round variety of regulars, the ones you always expected to encounter at Buddy's. The old man also usually ran into co-workers from the city, down on vacation or helping a relative work on his house. There was Vinnie, a short Italian guy one of whose four daughters married a guy who owned a boarding house in the older section of Point Pleasure. He still spoke with a thick Italian accent even though he lived his entire life in South Philly after coming to this country following his escape from the Fascists in his native country. Vinnie always offered a courtly bow when the bartender brought him his glass of wine.

And there was hard of hearing Wilmer, who towered over the old man but always stood up respectfully when my father met up with him because the old man was his supervisor. Wilmer always had to have things repeated, the old man explained, because for 'twenty-three years he'd run a machine on night shift. When an opening on maintenance came up on my shift, I requested him so I could get him away from that machine else he'd lose his hearing altogether'.

Guys like that always stopped by to see my father at Buddy's and, as he is a "regular", they came to be accepted as seasonal regulars.

One time with a number of this crew; Muldoon, Wilmer, and Harmon, my old man took his first fishing trip in a boat. As that expedition left Osten's Harbor on the west side of Point Pleasure, after a three hour "warm-up" at Buddy's, one could easily foresee the tragicomic results.

My old man loved to fish. He preferred to do his fishing from the beach. Muldoon always says that if God had wanted man to fish from boats he'd have given us oars for arms and anchors for feet. Muldoon hates boats. That was another thing he shared in common with the old man.

The sight of the two of them, under the influence, swaying and rolling along the floating dock to the rental boat, bobbing up and down in unusually calm Osten's Harbor, was worth emptying the bar on a hot sunny day. All the regulars gathered near the bulkhead as those four intrepid mariners loaded fishing rods, bait, empty cooler "for all the fish we're gonna catch" and full cooler containing cold beer "to drown our sorrows if we don't".

I wasn't there. My memory here is secondhand. But such vivid and thoroughly embellished recollections were offered later by the regulars that I can remember it better for being absent.

Muldoon fell in first. Harmon, supposedly the most seasoned mariner in the group, became a veritable Captain Bligh once he stepped aboard. He began waving his arms and knocked an already unsteady Muldoon overboard. Harmon began shouting at Wilmer, who couldn't hear much in the first place and even less as he was struggling to get the engine started. The regulars were whistling and cheering and raising bottles they'd smuggled out from the bar. Wilmer finally got the boat started but Harmon couldn't steer so they went 'round and 'round at high speed in a tight little circle that sent a wake over the docks and infuriated all the real mariner types in the marina. Then, with all eyes turned his way, the old man lost his lunch.

He'd already eaten it, mind you. So he lost it the hard way.

That afternoon earned him the nickname of "chummer", the explanation for which term is obvious for those of you who fish.

Having not wet a line; having not navigated their way out of the harbor; and with half the crew feeling under weather, the crew returned to port and marched back to Buddy's; followed by the derisively hooting and whistling regulars.

From that day on, the old man was an avid surf fisherman.

He laughs now as he recalls this first and last boat fishing trip with the crew from Buddy's. He fools around with a swizzle stick while the bar tender brings another round and then nods to Muldoon who had sent it down.

I decide that was a good time to tell him about my recurring dream, him having the benefits of eternal insights, which I assume is a form of x-ray vision. I describe my situation as being a kind of hell, where I'd been sent because I'd wasted all this life that I had but I'd never pursued my dream, which was to be a writer.

He frowns at that. He never liked the idea of me being a writer; never felt comfortable with it because he could never understand what it was a writer *did.* His idea had always been for me to get a nice cushy government office job and I could write on weekends if I wanted.

To him, writing is kind of like golf or fixing antique cars. Do it when you retire, hopefully with a pile of money to support such a 'bad habit'. I stopped bothering to discuss this subject with him after one or two gloriously futile attempts. But seeing as tonight is a special occasion, I figure I'd make another try.

"In this vision of hell, I'm condemned to write and rewrite this one sentence over and over until I get it perfect." He shakes his head, not seeing what the fuss is about.

I explain the myth of Sisyphus to him, about this character in Hades whose eternal punishment is to push a big boulder to the top of a hill and after struggling all day finally get it to the top. Then the day ends and the boulder rolls back down to where he started and he wakes up and finds himself at the bottom of the hill with the boulder.

"That *would be* a bitch." He agrees "Now, *my* idea of hell is waiting an eternity for my favorite bartender to fill my mug and he stands at the tap pouring but the beer never reaches the top and at the end of the day, he pours it out and has to start over the next day and my mug is still empty and I'm getting thirstier and thirstier."

The bartender gets the hint; gives the old man a sidelong look and brings us two refills.

"Ya know, when I got something really bugging me, it helps to take my rod and head down to the beach." The old man says wistfully. "Nothing quite gets out the kinks like a few good long casts and you're wading up to your waist and the waves crash and toss you around but you hang in there. It's a feeling..."

He pauses. The old man never waxed philosophical as long as he lived. Stuff like that, thoughts and feelings, were kept to yourself where they belonged. But this is a new father and part of this new father talks about his thoughts and feelings. Awkwardly and hesitantly; but he talks about them.

I understand what he's trying to explain. He never felt so much alive as when he was fishing. I understand because sometimes when I'm down there casting a hookful of squid as far as my arms will let me; knowing there's a fair chance that a killer bluefish will lash away at it and give me a half hour of primitive bloody fight...well, you don't have to be Hemingway to understand the purity of that feeling.

The old man actually manages to get the tear ducts working. With a Herculean effort he causes a solitary drip to course down his face. That tear washes away Muldoon and Harmon, the slanted floor, thick smoke and dim lights of the Buddy's Bar he loved so much.

The travels of that simple tear bent time until something snapped and I'm standing in Buddy's Bar, a brightly lit clean place lacking any of the grungy charm of its former self. It's new and improved Buddy's, part of the upscale renovations that had come with a vengeance to raise Point Pleasure out of its working class malaise and yuppify itself into becoming part of the brave new world of real estate bubbles and outsourced dreams. I'm not at all sure the old man would have approved and I sink warily away from some name card touting entrepreneur

The new Buddy's does have a fireplace, but there's a fake fire burning that gives false flickers and offers no warmth. And the new Buddy's has about a dozen of these high tech/high definition wide screen flat television sets all around the place so anywhere you sit or stand you can watch the big game, and watch you must since the sound from each set drowns out any possibility for conversation. And the new Buddy's has karaoke.

Some guy sits in a booth with a cordless mike and sings this sappy song to his girlfriend which is okay except everyone in the place has to hear it. The bartender mumbles disapprovingly that they actually raise drink prices while this is going on.

The floor is newly tiled and it's level. The tilt that once led you into the inner sanctum is gone and so are Muldoon and Harmon and all the others. In their places are some young guys smoking cigars, chortling loudly into cell phones and looking smug, like masters of the universe on holiday.

The old man is slumped in his wheel chair again and I realize that I can't leave him in this place. I'm recalled to what it is I'm supposed to be doing. I quickly wheel him out of Buddy's and load him into the car.

I speed across deserted Point Pleasure streets, past block after block of newly built condos each looking exactly like the ones before and the ones after. All the old landmarks have been razed to make way for this yuppie paradise. We finally escape under the boardwalk and onto the beach.

In the distance, I can hear the pursuit that we had lost when we first entered Buddy's. Relentless cops, television ghouls, put upon EMT's, followed by assorted stragglers and gawkers, screaming down the beach as I vigorously work at the trunk and get out our fishing tackle.

I load the old man back into his wheel chair and we shove off down to the water's edge. I park the chair and begin baiting hooks. The old man struggles mightily and manages to take in a deep breath.

The salt air works wonders. His eyes clear and his chest swells as that good salt air, full of popping ocean bubbles and good old fashioned unpolluted oxygen, courses through his lungs and pumps red blood cells squealing like a kid on the roller coaster, into his veins and arteries. I can see him blowing up there in that chair like an inflatable doll; growing with each pure inhale; coloring with each exhale of that accumulated poison from years stifling in the city.

I cast his baited line far beyond the breakers and he looks at me proud. He'd taught me how to cast. And I nod, ready to teach him, this time, if necessary.

I can hear the approaching commotion but the old man stares intently at the water, at his line, at the breakers, at a gull hovering over us laughing, at a ghost crab scuttling out of his sandy burrow while a herring gull swoops down and plucks him up for lunch.

The old man's head is swiveling about 360 degrees, taking it all in. An osprey hovers over the water; waiting and waiting then striking, immersing his entire body in the water.

We both watch forever to see if that intrepid hunter will rise out of that totally alien universe. Then we cheer lustily when he emerges, churning prey clenched in unforgiving steel claws.

Suddenly, without medical release from his attending physician, without giving it much thought at all, the old man is out of the wheel chair. He takes a ponderous step toward the sea. And then, just like that, he has a fish and it's bending the end of his rod into a jiggling pretzel.

The racket behind us is real close now. The old man purposefully strides into the water, working the reel, tugging back, letting go. I watch his arms swell. Blood really pumping into those arms as he tries to jerk the fish before it's too late. He's waist deep in the water as I nonchalantly turn to see flashing police car lights and hear the droning of helicopters coming over the crest of the dune.

I nudge the wheel chair into the ocean where wave upon advancing wave eagerly swallow it up and when last I see it, it is tumbling helplessly on out toward the continental shelf where it will hopefully find a better life as part of the artificial reef system.

I pop open a beer and watch. The Keystone Kops rush past, heading up beach. Two pause to watch the old man, sunburnt now and cursing up a storm of enthusiasm as he reels in a 38 inch striper, still jerking and fighting even as it dangles in mid-air, held aloft by the old man who asks how I could possibly think of getting a beer without grabbing one for him.

The cops ask if we'd seen any runaway invalid types. The old man laughs and drinks deep and says:

"Ain't no invalids here. Fishing's too good today."

The cops wish they could stay and fish themselves and have a few beers and the old man laughs.

"Somebody's gotta work for a livin'."

The fish lies motionless on the sand staring open eyed senseless in the sun.

"Did you see how that fish fought, son?" he asked, looking down in admiration at the striper. "To the very last. It didn't give up…even when it knew the odds were against it and it was hopeless to go on…even as it hung in the air lost out of water. It fought until it was truly tired and couldn't fight anymore and then it died quickly and with no fuss. That's how I want to go."

He didn't have to describe the unwanted alternative; hooked up to bottles and jars of chemicals in and chemicals out. Utterly dependent upon the well-intentioned meddling of loved ones and strangers. Unable to chew his food or eliminate his waste without the humiliation of needing help.

He looked over at me as he finished his beer. Both eyes were clear but we both knew that the inevitable fog would soon set in again. We both knew that he would not be going back. Here is where he would bid his farewells.

And that's how I prefer to remember him; walking steadily on his own two legs, powered by the force of his unrelenting will; straight and strong into the ocean where waves and currents lovingly carry him out to where the giants of the deep fared mightily. There to become part of the ongoing divine process of life. Rather than withering away to nothing, less even than an unsatisfactory shadow of memory, wasted within the confines of a disease-ridden city and trapped inside an artificial existence whose meaning is more capricious than the relentless tides.

"A Sugar Coated View"

It was with the waning of summer that Thorsen began waxing philosophical. Tottering precariously on a foot stool in the middle of the kitchen floor, Thorsen emoted for his captive audience, consisting of one tipsy, though skeptical girl friend.

Taking the Sermon on the Mount as his rhetorical point of departure, Thorsen's Diatribe from the Foot Stool departed from anything resembling coherence until only the most prescient theologian could detect any resemblance to its Biblical model.

Christ's references to birds was taken up by Thorsen and perverted to flies. It went downhill from there. Thorsen smote the air for emphasis. Actually, he swatted buzzing gaggles of insects as they paused for a rest stop in Thorsen's kitchen before heading south like everything else in Point Pleasure that time of year.

"Just like people." Thorsen pronounced, moving forward dauntlessly with his twisted metaphor." Consider their breeding capacities. Consider their single-minded determination to pester and annoy."

He paused to allow his audience to yawn nervously. The girlfriend was never certain where his oratory might lead.

"If a lowly fly occupies one designated space and a human, top of the food chain,occupies the adjoining space, there can be no coexistence. Not from one point of view, the fly's I mean. Such a harmony is incompatible with the fly's view of the universe and its mission in it. It is the fly's nature to occupy the human's space as well as its own. When the human feels the same way in reverse he is only acting out God's will."

Thorsen paused to take a deep swig from a long necked sixteen ounce bottle of domestic beer

"The fly's maker, probably Satan or one of his minions, imbued it with an exaggerated capacity and propensity to torment."

The girlfriend, stirring a bloody Mary with her right forefinger, wondered what had brought this on. Then she recalled igniting the flames of Thorsen's oratorical fire by nonchalantly mentioning that there were a few more flies in the house than usual.

Thorsen's eruptions had grown worse that summer. Ever since the lay-off. At least when he was working, he confined his ranting and raving to specific topics usually related to assorted lunacies encountered on the job. Now that he was idle, with time on his hands, an eye determined to observe, and a mind bent upon criticism, all topics were grist for his mill.

Hence, the lowly fly.

"Maybe they're heading to Florida for winter and just dropped in for a snack." She suggested feebly.

Summer had faded fast. For those living along the Jersey shore, Labor Day, the grand finale for tourists, had come and gone. All the suntan lotion was packed away. All the salt water taffy had been wrapped and stored in the dark recesses of closets to await Christmas when it would serve as gifts to less favored family members.

On cue, the hordes had reinfested their cities and shopping malls; abandoning those fragile ecosystems they'd overrun mercilessly for the three months of summer. Kids were back in school and annoying their teachers.

Thorsen lived in one of those rickety old Victorian ramshackles that no one in their right mind would build; proving that point by building it on the ever-shifting sands of barrier islands strung all along the New Jersey seashore. Sprouting in profusion along the coast at the turn of the last century, they had been products of the same generation of fecund minds that introduced automobiles, the airplane, and the concept of world war.

Thorsen viewed his domicile symbolically; man's rebellion against nature; an exhibition of capitalistic Yankee know-how with a generous amount of scornful Puritan nose-thumbing thrown in for those who preferred their beach scenes naturally pristine rather than postcards depicting man's dominion over nature.

What remained of the natural scenery, a string of scrawny man made dunes battered winter after winter as a message from the sea that dunes were not supposed to be there had already assumed a mellow golden hue as part of their autumnal aging cycle. Having loitered in those dunes, Thorsen had also adopted a golden hue; part of his seasonal aging process. Even though he'd been told by three dozen busy-bodies that his coloration would result in his face falling off or some other cancerous reaction to all that sun.

"Used to be sun was good for you." Thorsen mumbled.

The girlfriend shook her head and reached for the tomato juice and vodka.

They were all gone. The tourists and the well-intentioned neighbors and relatives with their words sympathy and encouragement. All back to their busy little worlds and their busy little lives. Unemployed Thorsen had the place to himself. And he had nowhere to go and nothing to do.

The job, which had paid outrageous gobs of money sufficient for him to settle outright in cash for the rickety house, was gone. Was he a victim of the global machinations of the dreaded and mystical Trilateral Commission or had the government with its NAFTAs and GATTs and other nefarious acronyms done him in? Had his job been whisked off to some call center in Bangalore, India? Was he just another white collar cipher, cast aside in still another mind-numbing corporate merger that was leading to one huge global conglomerate employing ten people: a guy with a computer and nine custodians to mop and dust around the enormous electronic brains of the outfit?

What had he done for a living anyway? If required to participate in one of those 25 words or less essay contests to describe what it was he actually did every working day for thirteen years, he'd come up 21 words short.

After 'Damned if I know' what could he write?

He had been one of those faceless, disposable entities who have come to overpopulate post-Industrial America with their confused and anxious faces, glazed by the dazzling pace of the ever-changing landscape; incapable of keeping up with that pace and forever falling behind. The truly BIG work had already been done and what was left had been farmed out to specialists working new magic in arcane little disciplines that the average Joe can't comprehend. While he bristled at the idea of being an average Joe, he conceded that he was part of the vast unwashed majority standing in a daze wondering what really did happen when the universe crossed into Y2K. Left out. Unheeded and uneeded. Obsolete. His reason for being having been outsourced

The age of individual heroics had passed. Today's true hero held on and survived and did his best to make sense of it all.

Thorsen didn't really hold with such a bleak philosophy but having plenty of time to brood over his condition, came to realize that brooding felt good. Day after day, the big highlight was the coming of the mailman and the hope of at least a form rejection letter in response to all the resumes and sunshiny letters he'd sent out in early summer when the bright promise of hope matched the June sunshine.

But then came the humidity and torpor of July and mornings spent making fewer contacts and less outgoing mail; turning into earlier and earlier trips to the beach until by summer's end he put in a longer day than the lifeguards.

The night before had brought the first cold winds out of the northeast and they had to sleep under a blanket. The girlfriend took the arrival of the chill as a personal message for her to get herself out of Point Pleasure. That morning, sunshine and fair winds had returned and she wanted to change her mind after two or three bloody Marys. Until Thorsen started his lecture.

Usually, she could conceal herself sufficiently in booze or daydreams to remain oblivious to his outbursts. He was eccentric. Bordering on daffy now. But she'd known him when he'd been stable.

When both were busy working, there had never been time to enjoy long talks and really get to know one another. Now she wondered how she'd manage to stay with this lunatic so long.

At the very moment that she entertained that thought, Thorsen was entertaining himself by nonchalantly slaughtering entire nations of flies that were suddenly everywhere.

Except for those moments when the girlfriend's participation was unavoidable, Thorsen had settled into the life of the hermit. He thoroughly enjoyed having no relatives, neighbors or friends about. Having detached himself from a world that had detached him from itself, he logically progressed to detaching himself from those who had been closest.

When summer entered its dog days in August, He took more and more to the indoors; inside himself, inside the white-washed mausoleum overlooking the sea except for infrequent forays out to the porch or even rarer hikes down to the water.

But now the weather changed and even those excursions would end. As cold rain began falling, it somberly tapped out in Morse code: 'it's over. Get out of here" over and over on the slate-tiled roof. The girlfriend understood immediately the message of the rain and she did precisely that.

She packed. Thorsen protested but his protests quickly weakened and he was soon helping her with the bags.

"The disposable Barbie girlfriend. You can't just walk out like this." He moaned with such obvious insincerity that the girlfriend had to respond to his sham/ham effrontery by pointing out that she could 'indeed, walk out.

"Afterall." in a tone of triumph, "I have a life'.

"It's just a little rainy period." He wheedled.

"That's what the people in Johnstown said just before the flood." She countered. "You need to be alone for a while. A few gloomy, rainy days alone in this creaky place oughtta cheer you right up."

Thorsen surrendered to feminine logic and shooed her out the door. Thorsen settled back with a shiver along his spine, to listen to the rain drumming its sinewy wet fingers on the leaky roof he had no intention of fixing.

Thorsen stopped kidding himself the moment her car had clattered down the shell drive way away from the house. He wasn't glad she was gone.

He loved her very much and was grateful for the way she loved him. She had given him wonderful experiences and had rescued him from the ragged edges of an adulthood that had been little more than extended adolescence with lots of cash and good credit. She had always been the one who made him behave responsibly; drawing him back toward the center from a dissipation that threatened to destroy him with the reckless pace of the dance it led him. He'd always wanted to be independent, free of the day to day worries of incrementally peddling one's self and one's precious time in order to keep the proverbial roof (leaking) over one's head. She had kept his nose to the grindstone until they took away the grindstone.

And now, he was out of that game and she was gone and he was peeking toward the edge again.

He realized how arbitrarily economics treated people. He had never been an adventurer even in his least inhibited period. Was not inclined by disposition or talent to be the primitive hunter of meat. Thorsen depended upon the artifice of organized society to protect him from the savagery of the real world. He understood now that economics was a savage philosophy

Without a meaningful skill to respond to any challenge beyond tumbling into bed at night and out again come morning. He thought about the time squandered carousing; the years of dodging responsibility; hiding from reality behind books, parties, music, movies, booze and all the other modern day drugs. Until finally settling into a routine that allowed him the false security befitting the "responsible" in modern society, only to be unceremoniously cast out.

He made believe that he was ecstatic that she was gone. There had been talk of children...the kind of serious talk that *really* underscores commitment to a specific life. But now, he was free again to do whatever he wanted.

He didn't have a clue what to do with himself.

Time passed. Point Pleasure did a Brigadoon; shrinking in upon itself in preparation for winter hibernation. Thorsen had no intention of immersing himself into the lifestyle of the local.

He had evolved into one of those cranks, delightful when enjoyed from a distance and only in small glimpses. He found his fellow humans annoying on their good days. But Thorsen based his assessments upon his own past relationships which had always been rocky and marked by misunderstanding progressing, quickly to animosity.

No matter what else he did during this transition period, he would NOT be establishing ties with the locals. He assumed that they would reciprocate.

People rarely did. Leave one alone, that is. Something seriously wrong with anyone who wants to be alone as much as Thorsen. Tongues wag. People have a talent for intruding into the most securely guarded places, clearly posted 'off-limits' places like the solitude of someone troubled who is seeking solace.

And having gained access, they meddle tenaciously.

Thorsen was determined that that would not happen to him.

It was a time to catch up on reading. His selection fell into no distinct categories. He was no specialist. He knew just enough about a variety of things to understand that he didn't really know much about anything. For Thorsen, reading was a form of passive resistance; a justification for non-action. Not inaction. Non-action. Thorsen was aggressive in his refusal to act, especially at times when action was most appropriate and the act required caused the greatest personal discomfort of contact with others.

Books offered refuge for the refined solipsist.

It was always easier to deal with words and ideas and the worlds presented in print than it was to wrangle with 'out there'.

Now that he had some uninterrupted free time, he hoped to do some thinking, too. not planning. That planning variety of thinking went hand in hand with concepts of involvement and responsibility.

There would be no thinking about retirement or settling down and raising a family and how to save for college and financing the second vehicle they would need to make daily soccer practices and orthodontist appointments.

Thorsen wanted to do some *real* thinking. About BIG issues.

As he sank into his beanbag chair and attempted to relax and empty his mind, he thought: *am I thinking now?* Afterall, he thought, *what is thought?*

So he used a significant chunk of his first truly liberated afternoon mulling over the true nature of thinking and thinking how great it was to luxuriate in such self-indulgence. It was the stuff of undergraduate life and picking up coeds at the campus pub with whatever the slickest line of bullshit was that particular semester.

It was while in the process of gorging himself on mental fudge, that he first became aware of the invisible watcher. Recalled from a childhood fable about guardian angels sitting by his right shoulder in blinding white robes and charmingly fluffed and tapered starched white wings (He recalled too the darker and far more interesting angel perched at his left shoulder...sinister...urging him to do what he really wanted to do in the first place.). Both always quite in view but fuzzy and able to slip around the corner of the eye just when you think you've caught them off guard and really get a focus.

If the true nature of thought was to conjure up spirits to add to his torment, he was just as glad to have had all those years of mindless activity in a white collar.

One night brought changes in the weather. The girlfriend called and warned him that there was a hurricane watch for the coast. He laughed and told her he'd keep and eye out for it. He thought of asking her to join him in the vortex of the storm; then thought better of it.

There was banging and rattling in the attic that night. But Thorsen slept the sleep of the just; knowing it to be nothing more than angelic prattling, the forces of good and evil bowling. Wager: Thorsen's soul. The game concluded with a resounding clap of thunder and high-pitched giggling. Thorsen wondered who had won; shrugged and rolled over to go back to sleep.

Next morning revealed no blowing winds or hurricanes. Just sunshine.

Summer had returned; thumbing its redhot nose at everyone who'd heeded the calendar. A handful of birds, the ones too lazy or too stubborn to skedaddle south, chirped him awake. A cricket that had taken up residence in the bedroom closet gave a few last minute clicks to advise of approaching day. Thorsen welcomed it.

What he did not welcome were the flies.

That morning, Thorsen awoke to sounds of buzzing about his head. Some flies, having survived his diatribe from the footstool, were seeking revenge. The flies, part of a kamikaze advance guard, strafed his face.

Thorsen loved being awakened in this fashion. He wanted to show his appreciation by sharing his morning newspaper with them. After several largely ineffectual swats, he clambered out of his bed. In true slapstick fashion, he stubbed his big toe on the dresser and broke into a jig across the room.

Thorsen waxed poetic; singing paeans to any god perverse enough to create a universe that simultaneously contained: toes, wooden dressers, and excruciating pain; and then ordering them to interact to create a Jerry Lewis skit.

Continuing his obscene psalm, Thorsen staggered into the kitchen.

He saw right off that he would have to wait in line for breakfast behind about two dozen flies that had somehow infiltrated through the screen door and were helping themselves to bacon and eggs.

Whistling nonchalantly, Thorsen sauntered casually toward the counter, newspaper concealed behind his back. With a resounding swoosh that would have looked and sounded wonderful if played back in slow motion, he crushed three flies. A second mighty swipe brought down two more.

This is easy, he thought. And fun! He began to feel like the brave little tailor of the children's story. A third blow brought down seven flies.

Peace restored to his kitchen, satisfaction felt at a job well done, Thorsen prepared morning coffee and tried to read about the world's morning disposition of guts and gore through splatters of his own world's morning disposition of guts and gore.

Over the years, Thorsen had become a voracious consumer of newspapers. As he immersed himself in the mundane routines of responsible adulthood, he came to live vicariously through the exploits and lunacies of characters he encountered in daily newspapers. The newspaper was an ideal place of concealment from meddlesome others.

But Thorsen turned vicious in his reading selections; choosing only stories depicting tragedy: murders, disaster, and assorted mayhem. After a morning of plague on the Indian sub-continent, famine in the Sudan, crime and grime in the big cities and terrorist bombings in the Middle East; Thorsen put down his blood-soaked newspaper and poured himself another coffee.

The flies were waiting. Reinforcements had arrived. Battalions had taken up positions on the screen door. Advance platoons had reconnoitered the kitchen table. Scouts were infiltrating the sugar bowl.

Outraged, Thorsen attacked vigorously. Flies were soon dropping like...Thorsen grimaced and pictured the invisible watcher, watching him and grinning.

"Dignity Thorsen. Always remember: dignity."

Flies scattered in all directions; dispersing to strategic points throughout the house.

"I'll hunt you down like the cowardly curs you are." Thorsen screamed.

Methodically checking windows to make certain the flies had no way out or in, he determined that they must be breeding or cloning new recruits somewhere inside the house. A chill ran up his spine and he heard ominous music. A few pesky flies he could handle. But an army of technology-enhanced super flies?

Thorsen hunched over to read the paper, waiting for their next move.

Two war stories and a mass murder feature later, Thorsen's cup was empty and needed refilling. The kitchen was now under siege. Flies on the screen door. Flies on the table. Flies rummaging through the cabinets. Flies making long distance phone calls as they established lines of communication. Flies raiding the refrigerator. It was D-Day in the Thorsen kitchen.

Though outnumbered, Thorsen was superiorly armed. Taking up his trusty newspaper, he stormed the battlefield. Swatting and cursing like a berserker in the full heat of combat, Thorsen far outpointed the tailor with each ruthian swat. Battered survivors buzzed his head; dive-bombing his eyes, nose, ears, hair. Thorsen grew angrier with each incursion.

Then came the sneak attack.

Flies came at him from behind. Swinging wildly in all directions, Thorsen fought gamely but at last was forced to retreat from the kitchen.

Despite countless casualties, the flies had established a beach head in the house. They had taken the kitchen.

Breathing heavily on the living room floor where he had collapsed, Thorsen now reconsidered his strategy; seeing the gravity of his errors. Though physically and intellectually superior, he had underestimated the flies' tenacity. He had shown he could be out-maneuvered; that he was vulnerable.

"The little imps will be ready for me next time for sure." He fumed, hands quivering with adrenal passion.

Flies plotting strategy indeed! He thought.

"Well I'll outsmart 'em. Some good old fashioned yankee ingenuity and I'll show them who is master of this house. Anyway, who needs the kitchen?"

Abandon the kitchen? He shrugged, he hadn't eaten in days. His vow not to leave the house had included food shopping. The world out there was just too dangerous to risk life and limb for something as extraneous as groceries.

"No food in the house…then I don't eat." He reasoned. "But they don't eat either."

But the thought of surrender, the notion of any concession to the flies, aroused the martial spirit in Thorsen.

"This is my turf, my home. Fifty-four forty or fight!" He raged, delighted with the coincident symbolism attached to his house address.

Feeling lightheaded with imperialistic looniness, Thorsen came up with an idea.

He retrieved the garden hose from the attic where it had lain, as the weeds relandscaped the grounds around once stately Thorsen manor. Connecting the hose to the bathroom faucet, Thorsen grunted pleasurably at his diabolical cleverness.

If the flies want the kitchen, he would render it useless by introducing copious amounts of water.

"Scurvy maggot brood, they hate the stuff." He cackled.

Creeping back to the kitchen door, he peeked upon the enemy camp as he slipped the nozzle into the room. He was disappointed. He had expected to find gangs of rowdy flies lounging at the table; swilling his liquor as they dealt greasy cards and sang ribald battle songs while laughing at their enemy's follies. The scene proved to be anticlimactic.

The flies had regrouped on the screen door. Their many dead littered the battlefield.

"Uncivilized heathens." He scoffed. "Don't even bury their dead."

The kitchen was filled with signs of the recent battle: blood smears, broken corpses, sugar granules everywhere. But the flies had gathered fresh recruits.

Taking quick aim, Thorsen blasted the screen door with a powerful stream of water. Hundreds of stunned flies wriggled in buzzing heaps on the floor. Thorsen had recovered the element of surprise.

"The tide has turned." He shouted, surveying the havoc he had wrought in retaking the kitchen, now a useless, water-logged wasteland.

Thorsen didn't care. High principle was at stake here. He had fought to recover what was his by divine right.

Thorsen left the kitchen. *His* kitchen. Entering the living room, the look on his face changed from sublime satisfaction to shocked chagrin.

The flies had outflanked him, a brilliant stratagem. While he had routed a token force left to distract him, the main body of flies had taken positions behind him in the living room. Outsmarted again! The ringing inside his head started coming at him from the telephone.

"How is everything? Hadn't heard from you." It was the girlfriend.

"Gee, I thought I'd taken that phone off the hook. And everything's just swell."

"When are you coming back to the city?"

"I need a few more days."

He was no Bob Newhart on the phone. There was no comedic banter. He liked his phone calls to be as short as possible. He had no wit to spare for disembodied bodies talking to him from across great distances about trivialities. Especially when there were flies to deal with.

"The American home is sacred." He announced solemnly, more for the edification of the eavesdropping flies. "I love you. I love you all and will be with you very soon."

Hanging up, he once more turned his attention to the task at hand. He heard tittering fly laughter as they playfully swarmed and swooped about his head. It was then that he knew that he had only one course in this escalating conflict: chemical warfare.

"I've been invaded; my personal space, violated. Abused and heaped with scorn. These flies just don't take a goddam subtle hint."

He felt perfectly justified in using all the tools of modern science.

"I have my rights. I've never invaded a dung heap, after all."

Co-existence was not possible. The flies had breached every rule of decorum. They were not invited guests. They were not paying boarders. They were invaders, encroachers, expansionists. They had to be treated accordingly.

He marched righteously to the attic, where he found a can of "Crush Fly", the sure-kill insecticide.

Thorsen emptied the can's entire contents in one thorough spraying of the house. Removing his gas mask, he held his breath and peeked through the clearing fog to glimpse the ultimate destruction of the fly army. Perhaps, he'd even be able to enjoy a few moments watching them in their death throes, writhing in agony.

The room was all clear. No more flies. He had driven them out. Thorsen had saved his sacred domain.

But that would be too easy an anticlimactic an ending for this little drama, Thorsen thought. So it was not a complete surprise when Thorsen heard a familiar buzzing sound past his right ear. Then, his left ear. Then the right again;, then left. Flies playing chicken with him.

Thorsen shrieked in anguish and ran to his bed. He frantically yanked the covers over his head, safely burying himself from head to toe. He had been routed and demoralized more thoroughly than Napoleon's army retreating from Moscow.

Except for the bed, flies ruled the house.

Throughout the morning and into early afternoon, he stayed under cover as the flies took possession. He heard them out there; buzzing about with the complacency of conquerors. They were waiting for him to show his miserable face, or a toe, and were ready to pounce. He understood that there would be no mercy given.

He pictured their swelling numbers, swarming around and onto the bed...waiting for a chance to devil him.

"It's what flies live for." He considered.

Thorsen decided to bide his time; make plans; and pray that he survived until dark.

It was hot and stuffy under those covers. Indian summer had arrived at the Jersey Shore and the sun was in full blaze. He could hear the faint honking of geese overhead; veeing south to Florida and winter at Disney World. There was something about that particular sound: the first migrating geese of Autumn. But the comfort of familiar sounds was in the past. All lost to a rabble of flies.

The phone rang. It rang for quite some time before the party at the other end accepted no answer for an answer. Unless, that is, a fly communications expert had intercepted the call. He chided himself for having disconnected the answering machine. He didn't suppose that flies took messages.

Gradual drowsiness with an increasing chance of unconsciousness was the forecast for Thorsen's afternoon. The soothing hum of a billion flies buzzing in unison soon lulled him into a deep sleep.

As Thorsen slept, things happened. He was tied to his own kitchen table.

A spotlight beamed down on him; illuminating his wriggling body.

"Bring on the Inquisitors. Up the vivisectors!" he shouted with feigned bravado.

He heard the hissing laugh of his invisible watcher as flies covered his face. These initiated a ceremonial fly victory dance. He was swooning with nausea but he bore the indignation stoically, in true prisoner of war fashion. After all, the invisible watcher expected him to show weakness. Thorsen intended to disappoint him.

Thorsen opened his mouth, intending to utter a momentously pithy sarcasm but a platoon of flies quickly scurried down his throat and ruined the moment.

Other flies discovered various entry ways to his innards and began roaming curiously about inside his ears, nose, eyes, and throat. They intruded like so many meddlesome specialists.

Vomiting was an appropriate response to these intrusions but, having fasted for the past few days, there was nothing in his stomach to bring up. Actually, his stomach was not empty. A muffled hum rose from his stomach into his throat. The flies had relocated and were setting up housekeeping The flies kept moving in like so many Steinbeckian Okies discovering California after suffering the indignities of life in the dust bowls of garbage pails. Finally, the stomach could contain no more. It burst. He knew it would happen. How many flies can a stomach hold? He considered the mess he had become. But then he pondered his feeling of detachment from the entire proceeding and consoled himself that it only be a dream. Even as millions of flies and their maggot offspring munched away contentedly upon his innards.

He tried to cry but those thirsty little buggers had drained all the water out of his tear ducts. Screaming wasn't possible either because flies had already divvied up his tongue to make picnic sandwiches.

He woke up at this point. Even though a still detached part of his psyche convinced its self he was dreaming, the imagery had turned too graphic for comfort.

He lay deathly still, listening. Hiding under the blankets.

He was covered with sweat from being under the covers throughout the hot day. Outside that womb, a rumbling sound shook the room. Peering out stealthily, he saw that billions of flies had convened all around him on the bed. A camp had been established with little maggots bivouacked everywhere. As Thorsen watched, morning rations were being distributed to the troops.

He was somewhat relieved to see no Thorsen tongue sandwiches. Instead, the flies supped on stale chocolate cookie crumbs, left over when his girlfriend's niece had visited in July. Ah, how he longed now to hear that child's shrill and insistent voice, dragging him out of his hammock for excursions to the boardwalk amusement piers and other venues Thorsen normally avoided. And the elephantine pitter patter of her tiny feet drumming across the floor each morning to announce the onset of another day's fun-packed activity.

He longed to see her come through the front door that very instant. Perhaps the flies would lose interest in him…

Feeling like Gulliver among the Lilliputians, he observed an impressive changing of the guard as a new squadron took up patrol points along the edge of the bed.

One impressive-looking fellow stood head and shoulders above the rest. Obviously better fed, he bullied the smaller flies and was pampered for no other apparent reason than because of his size and ability to vocalize. Many of the flies hovered on the brink of starvation yet they deferred to this individual whenever a morsel of chocolate chip cookie was carried forward. Thorsen further observed with a snide thought for the corporate classes among his own kind, how that worthy ate with indefatigable gusto and nary a twinge of conscience or compassion for his less fortunate fellows.

Has to be a CEO. Thorsen concluded.

The honcho wanted to parlay. Thorsen was given to understand this by the appearance of a white flag borne by an approaching delegation.

How does one talk to a fly?

Through a translator.

A fly that had spent its youth (approximately eleven frantic minutes) at a language school, stepped forward.

Fearless leader licked his chops and rubbed his forelegs together vigorously. Wants food and women, Thorsen thought. No, just food. Flies don't need women…or do they?

This was followed by a bellicose buzz. The translator informed Thorsen in a tinny voice reminiscent of Vincent Price in the classic movie immortalizing our particular insect that his position was hopeless.

Thorsen had to admit that it didn't look good but he wasn't about to concede anything to this garbage-breath. Outnumbered and surrounded. Superior technology and intellect had not succeeded. The translator smoothly pointed this out.

Then, he proposed a deal.

Winter was coming. Flies detest winter. It inhibits all of their favorite activities. Thorsen didn't want to dwell on what these might be; having enjoyed more than one human's share of interaction with the creatures.

The flies' reasoning buzzed this way. There was plenty of room in this drafty, rickety structure. The human would designate an area for the flies and fill it with enough sustenance to keep the flies catatonically torpid throughout the winter. If the terms were met, the flies would withdraw from their recently won territory.

This presented logistical problems. How to explain this arrangement to the girlfriend? How to get sufficient food in the house to feed the flies since he'd vowed that he'd never leave the house again? And how to explain bulk fly food (whatever that might be) to the girlfriend? He decided to try reasoning with the flies rather than explaining to the girlfriend.

"Do you ever watch television? CNN News? Read the newspaper?"

The flies rubbed their legs together violently when the latter, a weapon of mass destruction in their lexicon, was mentioned. Thorsen went on about the countless ways one can get hurt outside. He shared his thoughts about the invisible watcher and the many shapes death assumed.

The flies looked skeptical.

He then got into specifics; telling of Muslim terrorists and airplanes crashing intentionally into buildings. He spoke of burning cities and scud missiles gone awry and innocent hostages blindfolded and beaten simply for being in the wrong place, at the wrong time. He told of religious fanatics and ideologues of philosophical stripes across the spectrum who killed and maimed in the name of supposed ideals…all at the behest of their own version of the invisible watcher.

Now Thorsen became really animated. He spoke of derailed trains and sinkholes that swallowed automobiles and madmen who riddled subway cars with machine gun bullets because someone, sometime, somewhere had looked at them in a manner they recalled at that particular moment for no reason to have been offensive.

There were people, people right out there Thorsen gesticulated violently at the door, who stole and hurt and killed out of some desperate need they felt or imagined. People so crazed on drugs or booze or flipped out on some fantasy instilled by their very own invisible watchers that all sense of right and wrong had been obliterated from their psyches.

He tried to explain that these things happened because something was really bothering someone and they couldn't get a hold of it. And that something wormed itself deeper and deeper inside the person where it festered and grew, rotting as it grew, until it burst. Then, its billions and billions of tiny molecules traveled through the veins and arteries all through the body and mind and soul; causing the person to do all sorts of irrational things to himself and anyone unlucky enough to be around him; people who, incidentally were struggling to deal with their own sets of festerings and poisons.

The flies shifted uncomfortably from leg to leg to leg…

Thorsen lectured the flies about earthquakes and floods and volcanic eruptions and tidal waves and hurricanes and pestilence and viral outbreaks. He asked them to consider the possibility of an asteroid orbiting Jupiter coming unhinged from its cosmic wiring and plummeting down on their head as they innocently stroll to the corner 24 hour convenience store to buy a truckload of sugar cubes. All the while, the invisible watcher laughs and plans his next bit of mischief like maybe a sunspot to short circuit all the electrical equipment on the planet and cause global socioeconomic chaos.

The flies rolled and rolled their many eyes.

Wait! He shouted, really hot on the subject. There's a lot more. Stuff people do to one another just outside that door. Nuclear radiation that makes you glow in the dark as your hair drops off and your gums turn to mush and various parts of you fall in the street as you walk along. Or how about acid rain that kills trees and poisons the water. Or one of our communications satellites could go off program and come crashing down on the sidewalk just as you're walking by; pushing your kid in the stroller to the neighborhood play ground.

Then Thorsen got a cagey look. How about pesticides? The buzzing from the flies drowned him out. He nodded sagely, sympathetic.

"Now you're beginning to get the picture."

This top bug was of the hard-boiled variety. He greeted Thorsen's impassioned explication with a buzz of skepticism.

Thorsen was intimately familiar with skepticism and instantly recognized its expression, despite the obvious difference in species expressing it. Hadn't the girlfriend looked at him exactly the same way just before she left, as he patted her on the head and told her everything would be fine and things would soon start to make sense? Come to think of it, he'd offered her a modified version of much the same speech he'd just given the flies. Hadn't worked with her. Wasn't working now.

He agreed to the flies demands.

He disguised himself with a bulbous silly-putty nose and organ-grinder's mustache to avoid being recognized by the colony of rapists, muggers, murderers, terrorists, drug peddlers, arsonists, underworld and third world types that had gathered just outside his door. He avoided ambush by slipping out a second story window, sliding down a drain pipe, and scurrying behind one of the few bayberry trees on the island left unscathed by the Point Pleasure Public Works Department pruning crew. Then, hugging the ground, he slithered until he reached the safety of a sand dune. Seeing that he had outwitted the muggers, snipers, et al, he raced off the beach and down the street at breakneck speed.

He made it to the corner convenience store without incident.

The cashier behaved strangely though. She never took her eyes off him as she rang up numerous ten pound bags of sugar and three cases of maple syrup he'd hoisted onto the counter.

"Got one helluva sweet tooth." Thorsen explained, blowing fake mustache hair strands out of his mouth.

He made it back to the house without encountering any religious fanatics or mad bombers. Soon, he was pouring sugar into thousands of neat piles in various rooms upstairs. These he covered with generous dollops of maple syrup.

Just as he finished, Thorsen heard bells tinkling; their melody recalling the Edgar Allen Poe poem in all its singsong glory.

The bells announced the daily arrival of the vendor Thorsen knew as the Ill-Humor Man, a free lance loose cannon and underground merchant, who ostensibly drove his truck up and down the streets of Point Pleasure in order to sell ice cream and other frozen confections to local children.

The Ill-Humor Man appeared at irregular intervals, just when he was least expected and most uncalled for. Kids loved him because he had all the goodies their fertile twisted little imaginations could desire. They brought him their dimes and quarters and he gave them what he kept, hidden, in the back of the truck.

The Ill-Humor man was not your run of the mill ice cream guy. No tutti-fruiti twin pops in this freezer. Have a taste of double barrel shotgun instead. Want a fudge sickle? Ill-Humor man hisses. Try an AK-47 on for size. Like chocolate pops? Bite into one of my dynamite pops if you want more than just a blast of sugar.

The Ill-Humor man carried everything a modern kid, wishing to inflict significant damage upon any unsuspecting persons or societal institutions he or she deemed to have wronged him or her in any way, could possibly need. One visit with the Ill-Humor man and American teenagers were sufficiently armed to storm into Haiti, Somalia or the regional public high school.

Thorsen purchased four sticks of dynamite.

"What flavor?" Ill-Humor man snarled, showing a mouthful of gold teeth as he aimed a steel-toed boot in the direction of an urchin who was fingering a submachine gun off the discount rack. "Don't fondle the goods unless you're a cash customer." He bellowed, tweaking another youth's pimply nose with a pair of ice tongs as the youth attempted to shoplift a pair of brass knuckles. Ill-Humor man then turned to confront Thorsen but not before showing a bit of starched white fluff he had concealed beneath a black leather jacket, official Ill-Humor uniform.

"Maple cinnamon." Thorsen quipped.

Thorsen rigged the dynamite the way he'd seen it described in the website he'd downloaded from the Internet. Whistling show tunes to boost his sense of nonchalance, he casually opened the door leading upstairs. Gesturing grandly in welcome, he ushered in his new winter housemates.

The fly fuhrer buzzed agreeably as he surveyed the accommodations. Deciding that the terms of the treaty had been met, the flies took possession.

Once all the flies had relocated, Thorsen pushed the plunger.

The sun boldly shoved aside a cloud that had been obscuring its view of the Thorsen residence for the past few days. It poked a beam of bright light in Thorsen's eyes, just as the entire second floor of the rickety Victorian cottage exploded into the heavens.

Thorsen executed a sprightly jig as he pranced around the rubble, not a fly in sight. He tripped to a screeching halt when he heard furious buzzing and turned to face the Lord of the Flies, covered with pieces of flaking plaster and dripping maple syrup. Vengeance flashed in his many eyes.

Thorsen was tired, truly tired. He'd endured the fly game. He was now ready to move on with his life. Destroying the second floor of his white-washed Gothic horror house had released him from the burden of mental baggage that had been weighing him down.

There were once again resumes to be mailed, phone contacts to make, networking to mend, asses to kiss, odds and ends, flotsam and jetsam, and bric-a-brac and miscellany to attend to and reorganize into something once again resembling a life. Thorsen's mind raced fast forward into this new life he was entering. He would tear down the ruins of the white elephant and replace it with a quadruplex. Jacuzzi in every bathroom. Wired throughout for high speed Internet access. If he couldn't make his big comeback in the World of Work, he'd make his pile in the hectic schizzy world of speculative seashore real estate. He wanted the world to be his oyster again; not just an empty shell discarded along the water's edge.

Suddenly, he realized that he missed his girlfriend. He wanted to take her on a moonlight stroll along the beach and sip champagne and make mindless small talk and formulate plans for a long and happy future together.

He reached inside the tool shed and pulled out the bazooka he'd purchased from the Ill-Humor man earlier in the summer when he was having trouble with aphids. He fired one lethal shot. Kicking up his legs, cartoon character fashion, the fly leader dropped dead on his back, a white lily materializing out of thin air to symbolize his new life beginning in fly paradise.

"Ah closure." Thorsen crooned.

At last, Thorsen knew that he had won. He bathed himself in the warmth of Autumn sunshine, enjoying the peace of his backyard. *His back yard.*

He felt safe and free and back in control of his life.

He whipped out his cell phone and called the girlfriend, informing her that he'd been joining her shortly in the city…if she'd still have him.

"Just have to close up the house." He said, "I'll probably have someone look at the roof."

The girlfriend informed him that he'd gotten a call from a firm that was interested in interviewing him as soon as possible for a management level, information tech position.

There was more, of course. Small talk and intimate talk and idle blather about events in the world, real events in the real world. Thorsen chuckled and said he'd be there shortly.

Thorsen hung up with a belly laugh. It had been a while so he wasn't very good at it. The laugh sounded more like the groan of some mortally wounded mythical beast. But Thorsen felt good.

This fly business had allowed him to purge himself of some annoying personal demons. He felt lighter now, able to float above, around, and beyond all that day to day stuff that life threw his way and expected him to handle. With his new found attitude, he reasoned, he'd be able to employ perspective and handle things; maybe enjoy life again.

As he walked toward the still smoking house, he heard fire engines approaching from the distance. He'd handle it, he knew. Life would become manageable and good.

That queasy quivering in his stomach was the long unfamiliar fluttering feeling of happiness.

"Bring it on." Thorsen shouted, doing his best imitation Rocky underdog prevailing shuffle.

If only he'd spotted the man in the turban, floor length robes, and Foster Grant Wraparounds. The one toting a scimitar recently purchased for the price a barrel of oil from the Ill-Humor Man. The one lurking behind the screen door in what was left of Thorsen's kitchen. The one bearing truly strange tidings from the invisible watcher, who now and as always, acted his role as the proverbial fly in the ointment.

"Sifkin's Fence"

My son used to tell me that there are pockets of overlooked magic carried over from other times and left floating in random isolated places or some such nonsense. He says that if those forces are not somehow appeased or released, they can harm you. Ichabod Crane at Sleepy Hollow comes to mind.

It was the sort of stuff I'd come to expect from him; home all day doing nothing. Plenty of time on his hands to think up this gibberish, while I fought traffic and slaved from dawn to dusk trying to make ends meet, his ends as well as mine.

When he goes and tells me this, about magic and the like, I believe that his *ends* may never meet if you get my meaning. I picture him squatting on a floor, cross-legged, sickening sweet smelling strawberry incense burning to disguise the worst kept secret of all time: that he's up in his room smoking pot all day and, as he addresses me, does so between huge crunching gulps of onion and garlic flavored potato chips; all the while trying to look through and around me at the television; watching reruns of the reruns of "Gilligan's Island".

The last time we have this father-son chat, the work day had been a particularly rough one at the widget shop so when he starts ranting about these magic places, I say what needed to be said and he replies with more mystic Sixties hippie mumbo jumbo. Next thing you know, I have him lifted off the floor, pinned to the wall by the throat.

Out of nowhere, his mother comes screaming hysterically, cursing and wildly flailing…at *me*…with a broom handle. The police are called in and I have a restraining order against me. I'm barred from my own house. Wife and son not sure if they want me around any more.

The rules of Perspective compel me to admit now that it wasn't long ago that *I* was this hot-headed old man, set in my ways, pig-headedly sticking with good old-fashioned, wrong-headed ideas, despite the passionate and often heartbreakingly eloquent pleadings of my son to at least consider matters from another angle; *his* angle. I was the adamant one; convinced that the time-honored way….*my* way, my father's way, or the highway…was the only way as evidenced by its longevity of being the way.

I no longer recall specific issues. Whatever it was that led to this fragmentation of my neatly compacted, too tightly wound little universe doesn't matter now. Suffice it to say that I was challenged and when challenged I fought back, letting instinct take charge. But, my universe was ripped open and found by my accusers and if the truth be told, by me, to be lacking in substance. My wife sided with my son. *That* set me back on my heels, A direct frontal attack that forced me to retreat and reconsider. But not in the way that my son had hoped with his pleadings.

I reconsidered alright. Reconsidered the foundation on which I'd constructed this life of mine. I arrived at a conclusion: that I was dead certain that I was right in all ways and how dare anyone question, yet alone challenge that certitude.

So instead of surrendering to mumbo jumbo, I reconsidered my marriage and my family and my role in both. And then I walked.

I walked; slamming doors shut behind me. I kept walking, ignoring the anguished pleadings from those who had been closest to me and who had wronged me and who were now begging me to pause and reflect on what I was doing. But I was through with pausing and reflecting; through with marriage and the family; through with the whole cracked pot scheme of living in middle class respectability in the safe cocoon of a nuclear family. Now revealed as the soft underbelly of my life.

I instantly set out to cover that exposed vulnerability with a hard veneer of cynicism and indifference.

Truth is, I had never felt fully comfortable in these roles I had been playing and had always had a walking itch. When the other members of my tight family unit turned against me so easily, that was just the excuse I'd needed to justify a bolt.

Like lightning cast from the hand of a Greek god, I moved away from the city of my birth and childhood; away from the home I'd made as an adult, and the wife and family and network of friends and acquaintances. Tore my copy of the social compact to shreds; scorched it to cinders; and walked.

I didn't stop walking until Philadelphia had receded into a distant haze and I had meandered far afield in southern New Jersey; following the shoreline of the Delaware Bay. I passed through places long abandoned and forgotten by the 21st century until I arrived at a spot that had once been the prosperous oystering town of Shellbank. The town had withered away and dried up shortly after the oystering withered away and dried up, leaving little more than a bleached shell.

What hadn't been blown to the four corners of oblivion by an unceasing wind that blew in hot off the bay, had sunk into the surrounding marshes. What remained was a handful of hardscrabble farmer types whose main crops were honey and dandelions which they combined to make a peculiar tasting wine. There was also a small patch of tumbledown, once elegant Victorians that now poked sagging eaves out of the high marsh grasses landscaped with a few hardy wind-tortured cypress trees, many bleached dead white and all tortured into all sorts of grotesque poses; like sinners petrified by the severity of their crimes and condemned to remain at the scene of those crimes for all eternity, their sins bearing a shriveled fruit year after year; trunks and limbs all the while calcifying as they twist and writhe and groan in that merciless bay wind. Until a Final Judgment Day when they at last would be blasted back to the wretched dust which had pushed them into the world ages ago and sustained them just enough to enable them to survive until some moment of ultimate truth....

It was a newspaper ad that had actually led me to Shellbank. The ad asked for someone willing to preside over the daily commonplaces of a small senior citizens rest home. My initial telephone interview with the operator of the home seemed to have been designed to convince me that my best course of action would have been to keep on walking into the bay or turn around and head back to wherever I'd come from. So discouraging and bleak was the description of the place, its people, and the lifestyle. I would be utterly alone, and yes, he did use the word "utterly"; friendless unless I wished to consort with a society of "should be dead" ancients, lacking only the traditional shrouds to certify their status. But I was not put off.

On the day I arrived, the operator was passing through Shellbank on his way back to his townhouse at Margate; pausing only long enough to satisfy his curiosity about an applicant apparently willing to sacrifice his sanity to the place and its occupants.

In search of redemption, I was his man. I thoroughly convinced him of this with the deadened way I greeted his cheerful efforts to make small talk about deep sea sport fishing and the fleshpots and other temptations of summer at the Jersey shore. After a long and awkward silence, he offered and I accepted the job.

The rest home was the center of what passed for life in Shellbank; the only place where anyone resembling a living soul gathered. The farms and Victorians appeared to be abandoned; except at night when a dim light or two, glowing behind pulled shades and double-locked doors told of some nominal human presence. All I ever saw were the old folk.

A few were on the porch when I arrived. Not to greet me, though my coming was no doubt the highlight event of the social season in Shellbank. Each sat in a personal, isolated section of the porch which encircled the first floor. They did not exchange any words. Each rocked creakily.

Up the road a piece, a crew of state road repairers was finishing up painting a pair of solid yellow lines down the road's center. Their work stopped at the border of Shellbank. Two cars that had been fuming and sputtering impatiently waiting for the flag man to signal "go", zipped past the rest home with a hot whoosh of the oppressive air. Headed through Shellbank on some secret shortcut toward coastal areas.

"No pausing in Shellbank; just passing through…as fast as your automobile can take you." A toothless rocker quipped, without missing a creaky beat.

That had been my welcome to Shellbank society.

First time I saw them together, all two dozen or so, was a few days later at the home's historical club meeting. It was an odd gathering. No idle gossip prior to the start of the meeting. As the group collected, no one sat together. Empty chairs and invisible lines separated and divided one from another. About me, the newcomer, the unknown, the *youthful interloper*, there was a repulsing aura that caused each to cringe and squint and shrink away into the darker recesses of the room.

The club has a presider. He wasn't a president in the usual sense of a club's having a leader figure. The presider was as reluctant to emerge from the shadows and man the helm at the podium as anyone else in the room. But, as if by unspoken command from the assemblage, when the designated start time for the meeting arrived, the presider wordlessly shuffled to the fore and cleared his throat. The already quiet room assumed a death-like stillness.

He mumbled over some notes, peering fixedly at his shuffling papers, as he monotoned about some incident related to the Revolutionary War that had been apparently long since mined for any shred of interest and was now a matter of repetitious necessity to lend some purpose to the gathering.

After droning on for some time about the significance of the incident on local fishing three centuries ago, the presider turned his attention to a thin pamphlet at his elbow on the podium. He nudged it with his elbow to make sure it wouldn't bite. He looked about uncertainly, as if hoping someone from the audience would rush to his rescue and bear the unholy thing away. Finally seeing no choice but to acknowledge its presence, the presider nodded at the pamphlet and, while still not actually touching it, expressed tepid thanks to "young Will Dietz".

Wilfred Dietz, one of the younger ancients but still stooped by many years shuffling around Shellbank, had researched, written, and designed the pamphlet. He had compiled a listing of the families of Shellbank and their lineages. Normally, I would have thought that such a personal "family" history would delight older folks such as these.

But not this group. They shifted uneasily in their seats as the presider made it clear that the club had neither sought such a history nor did it now appreciate the existence of such a document.

Reading through Dietz pamphlet, I learned something that struck me as peculiar. There were no children listed for the current residents of the home or anyone then living in Shellbank for that matter. I thought this oversight was caused by the egocentrism of bitter old timers resentful at being abandoned in such a place as this while their offspring frolicked about enjoying the varied and abundant fruits offered by the rest of the world.

As I skimmed through the pamphlet a second time, I realized that there *were no children or grandchildren.* Period. None existed. Shellbank's current crop of humans was its last. In fact, Wilfred Dietz *was* the youngster of the community.

Excluding yours truly, of course.

As the presider began to go into what he expressed to be the multitude of errors in Dietz work, the other relics suddenly came to life; that life assuming the form of snickers, guffaws, and sneers. All chroused in agreement that Dietz had wasted his time and was now wasting theirs. From my seat, I cynically concluded that time here was little else but wasted.

But I said nothing. Nor did Dietz, who suffered alone, stoically, two rows back.

I kept my head down, lest their nasty barbs prick me. I continued studying the pamphlet, concentrating on the section in which each resident was asked to provide his/her most "significant memory" from a lifetime lived in Shellbank.

Time and again, there were references to a place or landmark called Sifkin's fence. The memories expressed were not very memorable, or very clear for that matter. But each offered a comment involving this Sifkin's fence.

I put aside the pamphlet and tried to focus on what was being said but the level of abuse had become vitriolic to the point of becoming violent. I was embarrassed for them.

Finally, I couldn't handle their vulgar and obscene hoots of derision. Dietz had melted into his seat and was about to vanish altogether.

"I'm new here as you know." I started.

They turned evil old eyes my way. The presider gave me a sidelong glance and leaned against the podium in a pose that spoke volumes on these ancients' attitude toward anything that did not share the bond of common decrepitude: contempt. I recognized the pose. It was the same one I'd assumed during one of my last conversations with my son as he jingled his beads and mumbled about running off to Canada to evade the draft.

But I continued my address, assuming as pedantic a tone as I could under the circumstances as the old ghouls disregarded me and collectively shrieked and slithered in toward Dietz for the kill.

"I don't want to get off on the wrong foot here. But I'm a writer and I know how hard it is to sift through material to put together a piece like this. I think Mr. Dietz ought to be commended for his effort."

I stopped. I wasn't getting the reaction I'd expected. Instead of feeling badly about the way they were behaving, the ancients turned their anger and resentment toward me. For butting in. For being young.

Even Dietz glared at me. What made matters worse is that I lied.

I'm no writer. I had no idea why I said what I said except that I felt bad for the old guy and didn't know what else to say to help him.

No, it wasn't that. I said it because I wanted to get a rise out of these old wrecks and show them up for their display of bad manners and ignorance.

No, it wasn't that either. I said it because I was feeling bad for me. A third their age and here I am, as mediocre and bitter and alone as the oldest, creakiest relic in the bunch.

Then, I really stuck my foot in my mouth. "Could any of *you* have done better?" I sneered. No one cared enough to rise to that challenge. It wasn't fear. It was the sublime indifference of the truly aged.

"I'm reading these little remembrances you have in here. There are some interesting items that perhaps Mr. Dietz could have explored a little more deeply."

It was then that I mentioned Sifkin's fence. Everyone who had chosen to share a recollection had made reference however vague, to Sifkin's fence. Dietz had made no attempt to elaborate on who Sifkin was or what this place was or why it held so central a place in the heart, albeit a rotten heart, of this community.

But as innocuous as the comments in this history had been, the reaction in that room when I mentioned Sifkin's fence was electrifying.

The presider loudly gaveled me out of order. Chairs went flying every which way as the ancients climbed over one another to determine who could get the farthest away from me fastest, without leaving the room. A bank of low dark thunderhead clouds ominously rolled across the bay, coming to rest directly over Shellbank, the rest home, and my seat in particular. The clouds were greeted with sharp, knowing looks from the others; looks full of gleeful malice.

Then came a chorus of cane rapping and walker squeaking as the meeting came to an abrupt close and everyone rushed for the door.

"Wait!" I persisted, with the bullheaded witlessness of youth. "This Sifkin's fence is obviously an important symbol to this community." I stumbled, trying to somehow appease them. "Perhaps it's a cherished landmark, something that recalls a simpler time."

The presider could have sided a barn with all the hammering he was doing.

"Perhaps if our young caretaker were not so presumptuous as to try to impose his views without having the benefits of experience and knowledge about that which he speaks, he would be more temperate of tongue." The presider hissed.

I certainly shut up at that point. Dietz shook his head vigorously, waiting two rows back as the walkers shuffled and wheel chairs rolled and canes pecked their ways out of the truly adjourned meeting.

"I was always the impetuous youngster upsetting everyone at these meetings until you came along." He guffawed harshly when we were alone.

"What did I say?"

"Sifkin's fence."

"They mentioned it in your book. I figured it was some sort of lover's lane rendezvous or something."

"Or *something* all right." Dietz croaked as he slouched out toward the television room. "I guess you'll be revising my history. I can't wait to read how it turns out"

"I guess so." I couldn't help noticing how relieved Dietz looked.

"Well don't count on getting a lot of cooperation." Dietz said on the way out.

"Do yourself a favor young man. Forget about Sifkin's fence and worry about getting more variety on the breakfast menu than oatmeal and poached eggs."

Dietz was right. No one wanted to talk to me. When I tried to make small talk at lunch or before teevee hour or after evening prayers, they avoided and evaded me with an agility and speed that belied their advanced years. Some were downright rude and adamant in insisting that being rude and hostile was an entitled prerogative. Those wishing to handle me more gently put me off and said they had things to do.

I was never to see anything being "done" in Shellbank.

So one morning, I walked. But this time, I walked with a destination in mind: Sifkin's fence. I wanted to find out what it was, where it was. And I wanted to learn what hold it had on these people that made them so fearful to talk about it.

Sifkin's fence, I was to discover, was a broken-down, all but vanished cedar pole fence surrounding a patch of overgrown weeds on the other side of what remained of the tracks of the long deceased South Jersey Railroad, just at the edge of this bustling metropolis. Inside the broken circle of Sifkin's fence was a crumbled house; with caved in cedar shake roof and the emaciated skeletons of two or three shutters hanging on desperately from windows that hadn't contained a pane of glass since the administration of Franklin Roosevelt, the last president who mattered much to folks hereabouts.

What great hold could this fence and the place it encased have on these relics?

Of course, I was intrigued, as much by the nonchalant eeriness of the place as by the fact that there wasn't anything else to intrigue me at this point in my life. The fact that my interest united the community for the first time in ages in common dislike for a new enemy and all communication with me was reduced to cryptic monosyllables, punctuated by icy silence only raised the level of intrigue.

So I mounted my trusty bicycle, with much fanfare and bombast so that all the world of Shellbank would take note; and pedaled the hot, deserted road leading to Cape May Court House and the main branch of the county library. There, I planned to do some snooping into the history of this taciturn little community of living relics which had found new life in making me its anathema.

I rummaged through the yellowed records of the county, which go back to well before the American revolution to a time when Indians and whale fishermen were its only human inhabitants. The Indians left, not understanding or appreciating the cunning subtlety of the white concept of private property. The whalers left shortly thereafter; having pretty much depleted what there was of the local resource and seeking better opportunities in New England, where Herman Melville later immortalized them.

Then through the pages of local history, the usual cast of pioneers and settlers followed. Farmers, fishermen, hunters, woodsmen. They hacked out a way of life in a place that was surprisingly generous in the way of tillable soil, seasonable climate, wood products, fish and game.

It's ironic, given what progress, with tourism as its driving force, has done to the surrounding area, but the fact is that in that pre-tourism era when the great cities were springing up not far away in all directions, Shellbank was an idyllic place.

So much for background. This quiet, rural setting remained quiet and rural for a long time. Through the revolution and the establishment of our estimable republic; through the growing pains of the early 19th century; even unnoticed through the great upheaval of the Civil War.

It was after the Civil War that the Sifkin family came to live at Shellbank.

Henry Sifkin's father had been a fairly prosperous bay man on the Chesapeake prior to the Civil War. At least, he was as prosperous as it was possible for a black freedman living in a pro-slavery state to be at the time. Sifkin's father was an enterprising man. More importantly, he was no fool. He insisted that his children learn how to read and write.

Maryland, in a time of Civil war fought ostensibly to end the enslavement of black people, might not have been the most hospitable place for an ambitious man whom many white folk thought should be wearing chains.

Henry Sifkin's father could handle himself. He worked harder and for longer hours, than white men in his occupation. He commanded their grudging respect and, as a result of his own efforts, earned a good living from the bay.

But the life wore him down and slowly ate away at him. He worried about his family. He swore that his children would not have to struggle the way he had.

More than thirty years after the last official shots of that war had been fired, Henry Sifkin's father moved his family to a new community in New Jersey at a place called Whitesboro. He brought his boat and his livelihood, from the Chesapeake Bay to the Delaware Bay.

I read about George White, a Negro Congressman from North Carolina, and his effort to establish a community in the North where Negroes could enjoy what had been supposedly won on the battlefield. I didn't learn if Sifkin had been acquainted with George White or if he was part of the original group to settle in New Jersey. But there is a Sifkins listed as living in Whitesboro.

However, he didn't stay very long.

Reading between the lines of dried out historical record, I guessed that Henry Sifkin's father wasn't the community type. He was a loner. Independent as a Chesapeake bay man, he set out to find the same type of life for himself and his family on the new bay he made home, the Delaware.

He succeeded, settling in the vicinity of a hamlet of farms having a modest Baptist church as its "center" and a dirt road that passed nearby and eventually connected with a wider road that eventually headed in the general direction of Camden. Good old Shellbank hasn't changed much through the years, I mused.

Henry Sifkin's father died shortly after he'd settled at his new home along the Delaware Bay. But he'd managed to establish himself as a successful oysterman and he managed to teach son Henry the many tricks of navigating through the hard life on the water. He also made sure that Henry knew how to read and write because the father wanted his son to go on to "better things". But Henry was a stubborn man, as determined as his father, and elected to become a "man of the water".

Stubborn sons and disappointed fathers. How history takes us 'round and 'round. I didn't read that in the dusty archives of the county library. I imagined it; creating my own little history out of the dried snippets the yellowed pages offered about the likes of the Sifkins family. But after all, history is a story tailored by the mind's eye to suit the temperaments of the reader.

I *did* read that Henry Sifkins married a young girl named Sara Spaulding who came out to Shellbank from Whitesboro. It was then that, using the white cedar that was still relatively abundant, Henry built a modest house on the outskirts of the hamlet. It was the remains of that house that I had visited earlier.

A short while after the Sifkins had settled on the fringes of Shellbank, the railroad came through; snaking a line down along the western edge of the Sifkin property. It was this line that would link the Atlantic coast with Camden; and through Camden, Philadelphia; helping to cut the expense and travel time involved with shipping cargo and people from the coast to the city by ferry via the Delaware Bay. The railroad line greatly benefited Henry Sifkin's fledgling oyster business.

Convincing the railroad to locate a stopover at his place, Henry Sifkin was then able to ship fresh oysters to the city, wrapped in burlap and stored in great iced barrels. His business prospered and grew. He was able to hire members of the community. He was then finally and reluctantly accepted into the Shellbank community, a magnanimous gesture made none the less ironic by the fact that Henry Sifkin was by far its most affluent citizen and employed many of the locals at his ice house and on his oyster boats.

"Accepting" Henry Sifkin was no doubt made more palatable to the movers and shakers of Shellbank by the fact that he was rarely at home, preferring to spend most of his life on the water.

He did manage to stay on shore long enough to father a son, George.

The county records tell of the birth of George to Sarah and Henry Sifkins, with the birth taking place at home. It gives a date and a description of George as male and Negro. After those statistical entries, the record goes silent.

But the birth of George Sifkin, near the start of the 20th century, marked the appearance of Sifkin's fence.

I figured I'd start my interviews with one of the men. There had been one who seemed livelier and less hostile than the others. Potter had actually looked at me without a defensive scowl when I first announced my intention to supplement Dietz research efforts. Glazed indifference was more his game face.

A sun-browned face. Potter was a fisherman. The weathered leathery look and feel of the skin was my first clue. Then there was the tan line that stopped at the sleeves and neckline of his shirt and the cap that covered a grizzled white crew cut. Potter was clean shaven and bright-eyed.

He was shaving with a straight-edged razor when I came to his room for our interview. I started off by noting that I hadn't seen a straight-edge razor since I was a kid and a moldy Italian barber on our street corner used to shave my neck after every haircut before applying talcum powder and I remember it's being the best feeling in the world.

Potter stared at me blankly while I raved about this Italian barber and when I stopped, he grunted and resumed shaving, watching himself in the mirror as he carefully scraped the blade over his already smooth chin.

"Used to be drum fish and black fish in these waters, so thick you could walk acrost to Delaware. Some of 'em big as torpedoes from a submarine." He observed, nodding at my pen; his signal for me to begin taking down his remembrances.

"Clam and oyster too. You could reach down to the bottom with the nets and come up with full ever' time. Any fool could make a livin' on the water in them days."

I could tell by his tone of voice that the "fool" in question was not himself. I wondered what time period he was referring to as "them days"; whether he was talking about any of the Sifkins or merely reminiscing.

"Old man Sifkin was an oysterman and a good one. A lot of men hereabouts worked for him one time or another. He always knew where the fish were, no matter what the season or the weather."

"Has a son named George. George was why that fence was built in the first place." Potter now settled back comfortably in his chair, confident that he had hooked his quarry. I scribbled busily.

George Sifkin helped his father haul firewood and the burlap bags full of oysters when the boats came in. But George couldn't do much more than that. An "idiot", a "retard". The youngsters had other names for him, even less kind, but the fact was that George Sifkin was not capable of taking care of himself and had to be supervised constantly. That meant confinement.

"George wasn't allowed to play with the rest of the kids." Potter continued. "It wasn't so much because of him being a colored. He was peculiar. We'd go down in groups to the Sifkin place just to watch him on t'other side of the fence. Sometimes, nothin' happened. Sometimes, the strangest things."

Potter admitted that the children, himself included, often teased George Sifkin but Sifkin was so "gone in the head" he never seemed to notice or mind it. One day, Potter recalled, the children had been treating him real bad when George came close to the fence and tried to say something to them, tried to show them something. The youngsters began throwing empty oyster shells at George from one of the nearby piles.

"We didn't know any better. Or care." He acknowledged. "We didn't think he had sense enough to feel anything."

"Our aim was good. Near ever' one was a hit. And those shells was hard, some had pretty sharp edges too. Soon, George stopped dodging and just stood there. I ferget who 'twas, Bobby Dietz maybe, older brother to Wilfred who you was talkin' to at the meetin'…anyhow, he threw an old thick oyster shell that caught George good on the right cheek." Potter shook his head slowly, his voice assuming a far-off timbre. "Sifkin just stood there and looked at us a long time, blood streakin' down the right side of his face. Finally, we could all see a solitary tear move real slow down the left cheek….seemed like it took an hour to make its way down and we all just stood there stone still and watched."

"He knew. He understood what we was doin'. Mebbe even why we was doin' it."

When Potter saw that tear, it was a revelation. While he didn't admit as much to me, I could tell by the tone of his voice that he felt something akin to shame.

But that never stopped him, or any of the others, from continuing with their abuse in the days that followed.

Suddenly, Potter became more animated as he recalled George Sifkin's dog. A golden retriever, a beautiful dog none of them had ever seen before and none could ever say where it had materialized from that afternoon. Had to have come from under the house, Potter shrugged still unknowing. Must have been cooling itself in the shade.

"George, he turns away from us and starts playin' with this dog. All our shoutin' and shell tossin' had no effect. Him and that dog played fetch and tumbled about and paid us no mind. It was like there was nothin' beyond that fence and just him and the dog in the whole wide world."

It wasn't until later, Potter continued, when he went home and mentioned the dog at the supper table that his papa had snapped something about the Sifkins not having a dog. Henry Sifkins wasn't fool enough to trust his idiot son with any kind of animal.

But they had all seen that dog.

Potter and the other children had been spooked by that and other things like that that they had witnessed in their many visits to Sifkin's fence.

"Georgie could do things like that on his side of the fence. He wanted a dog there, there was a dog there. I don't know how to explain it." Potter rasped in a voice, now turned fierce, defying me to disbelieve him. "He had powers. We never tried to understand him; never tried to cross that fence. We just knew he didn't belong in this world."

Potter slumped in his chair, breathing heavily, as though the strain of the telling was more than he could handle. He angrily brushed aside my attempts to question him any further.

"On a time, whales came up the bay this far. And after a day's killin', the beach would be stained red and carcasses ever'place. The air was thick with flies feeding upon those bloated carcasses. Now that was a time, long before Sifkins and the fence. A time when life and death both held sway in this place and folks were sure which way the world turned and knew the seasons and the reasons why things happened as they did."

Potter pulled his fishing cap tight over his forehead to shield his eyes from the noonday sun as he slammed the screen door and went off to check his crab pots, down by the bulkhead; expecting to find nothing, as usual.

I didn't necessarily want a female perspective but Sally had flirted with me one morning as I served orange juice and corn flakes so I thought I might have a chance of getting her to talk. When I suggested as much, she invited me to her room.

There, I found her putting on make-up and fussing with her hair. I'm not sure why she bothered. No one ever came calling and no one here ever went anywhere. She took great pains to make herself look as much younger as the miracles of cosmetological science and the art of grooming would allow. She did it for me, I guess.

She stared at herself in the mirror for a long time after I asked about Sifkin's fence. Considering what, if anything, she was going to say to me.

Finally, she told me in a whisper about a hot summer day, just like today and every other day at Shellbank, but long ago. (You know), one of those days when there's nothing to do and a pesky hot breeze giving no relief; only riling the 'skeeters.

Folks just sat on their porches and stared; trying not to move too much. Just fanning themselves and waiting for sundown and, God willing, a break from the heat. The only sounds were flies buzzing and the creek, still and muddy, sizzling as it dried up.

"I went for a stroll and happened to find myself passing by the Sifkins house." Sally recalled, trying to sound daintily wistful but coming across more fragilely wheezy. "There was George playing alone in the yard the way he always did, no matter what the season. But on his side of the fence, there was snow." She paused for dramatic effect, and satisfied that she had my full attention, went on. "There he was, running and laughing, talking to himself as the snow fell and the ground was covered and he tossed handfuls of snow into the sky."

"He spots me and bends down. He comes up with a snowball. He throws it at me. I just stood there, waiting for it to hit me. Truth to tell, it was so frightfully hot, I was hoping it *would* hit me….But the snowball melted and vanished just as it reached the fence."

Sally paused, wondering if she had said too much; searching my face for reaction.

"I know it sounds crazy and, of course, I never told a soul because you know how folks are 'round here with their malicious gossip. Anyhow, George went back to his play like I wasn't there. So I continued walking."

"That's what I mean. Things like that were always happening near Sifkin's fence. Lookin' back, I suppose we all had saw strange things, had strange things happen to us; but no one ever talked about it." She paused, giving me one of those demure silent movie heroine looks. "That's what probably caused the trouble."

I had to lean in real close to hear those last few words as her voice had dropped and was barely audible. She had a frightened look on her face and she kept looking around the room anxiously, like she was afraid others in the home were listening and were even then gathering at her door, ready to burst into the room to tear her apart for saying too much.

Half joking, I tiptoed to the door and opened it a crack. "Peekaboo." I grinned, stepping aside to show her that we were alone, no eavesdroppers. She shook visibly in relief. But she did not resume talking until I had shut the door and taken a seat very close beside her.

I watched a swirl of dust motes dance in the light coming into her room, speculating on what dust is and what it can do, and what it was and what it might become with the proper amount of time and a certain set of circumstances. Then I considered that this was a line of dingbat thought I would expect someone like my son to pursue; luxuriating in ease and idleness as he waited for natural processes to create in him a perfect candidate for a place like Shellbank. My reverie was interrupted when Sally cleared her throat.

"You see, there was a little girl..." she began.

I left the room over an hour later, as white and shaken as Sally.

There was a ringing in my ears after I left Sally's room. It turned out to be the unfamiliar music of the home's official telephone, announcing a rarity in these parts: an incoming call. None of the residents showed any inclination to answer the call; none of them expecting any but the "final call". Therefore, it was left to me to stop the incessant ringing of this Poesque bell.

The call, it turns out, was for me.

My son had tracked me down and was calling me...collect...from some place that sounded far away. Canada? Canada had become a favorite point of destination for young men of my son's philosophical persuasion during our national crisis in Vietnam.

I didn't ask where he was and he didn't volunteer the information.

"Surprised to hear from me dad?" He asked, more than a trace of sarcasm in that voice I'd come to find so annoying.

"Delighted as always." I pushed the words out through clenched teeth. "Although I'm sure the call keeps you from more pressing business."

I could hear loud rock music blaring in the background and the sounds of clacking billiard balls. I pictured him slouching at a pay phone, half-swilled bottle of beer in one hand, pool cue in the other, phone cradled under his unshaved chin.

"Dad, can there be peace between us?"

I further pictured him, wearing sunglasses even though the bar was as dark as a tomb. I saw his long hair tied back in a greasy pony tail, which he nervously tugged at while bouncing from foot to foot unable to contain his nervous energy. He was so strung out on drugs and alcohol and adolescent angst. That was his life that I saw, along the merry path he'd chosen to take, after renouncing all that I had worked for to provide for him. I continued to see him, in his faded jeans of many patches, his velveteen jacket that had long lost its clownish sheen, his banged up hat. There he was in some time warp of his own, reading his own bad poetry on street corners in hopes of scrounging together enough loose change to underwrite his glorious brave new world lifestyle.

That was how I saw him. I could not understand what he was doing or thinking and he frightened me well beyond the point of mere generational revulsion.

I was never good at hiding my scorn and I had given up pretending that I cared.

"Peace, pot, and microdot, eh son. Let love make the world go 'round."

"As you say, old man, as you say." I could hear him deflating, picture driblets and fragments littering the barroom floor. "You have a lot of misdirected anger boiling away your heart and soul, dad. I feel sorry for you. Some day, that anger will burst out once and for all and most it will take you in most inappropriate directions. You should look for your bliss and let it release you."

"Is that some of the psychology I paid a lot of money for you to learn before you dropped out of college?"

"You win dad. Well, gotta go." He paused long enough for me to hear a throbbing electric bass, followed by the high-pitched squeal of a girl's laugh. "I just wanted to let you know that I love you."

"Love is all you need." I said/sang before returning the phone to its receiver.

I don't know what it is about the person he's become that angers me so. It's not the way he looks or acts. Everyone looks and acts strangely these days. It's fashionable. I certainly understand his wanting to fit in. It wasn't his politics, the protests, the rejection of everything I had come to represent that irritated me either.

His head was filled with romantic notions, typical for an inexperienced youth trying to figure things out; typical of someone who hasn't had all the feelgoody sentiments about one's fellow man stamped out by long-term exposure to the antics of the species. That was to be expected. Life had yet to disappoint him. Maybe I envied him for his unabashed innocence but I didn't resent him for that.

What angered me was his insistence that there was still possibility beyond the everyday routines that direct us; his unnerving pursuit of those pockets of "magic" he prattles on about, like there is some source of energy existing outside the preponderance of reality and inside these pockets those who are privy can harness this energy to help them overcome whatever it is that is hurtful, including the tendency to stay on the life path of least resistance.

He'd actually rattled off something like that to me one time, but I was only half listening. Such nonsense never pays the mortgage. Instead, I insisted that life swallows whole those who are different and treats with utmost cruelty those who insist upon trying to keep to a special path of their own making.

That had all come out during that last of those heart-warming father/son chitchats. Our dialog on that occasion ended with him telling me I was cold and unfeeling and with me scoffing that I would never stand in the way of his seeking his magic places so long as his search carried him away from my door. From there, our exchange went downhill, fast.

We did achieve a clarity of sorts; defining who we really were in relation to one another. Finally, when our anger crossed the line into hysteria and the potential for violence, my wife got into the act. She, naturally, rose to the defense of her only son; an act that pretty completely defined *her* for all concerned.

And when confronted this way, with such undeniable truth, I had walked.

I walked again, now; the voices still coming through the phone lines directly into my head becoming too much to bear in the confinement of the home.

As if on cue, moonlight appeared to guide me. A golden beam illuminated the path leading upland from the home. I understood right off where the beam wanted to lead me, so I followed it to the Sifkin place.

I stood rigid for a long time, enveloped in the sheer silence permeating the place. Was that music I heard? It was crickets, all around me, crickets.

Then, even the crickets were still.

I caught a flash of shadow from the other side of the fence and, for an instant, thought I saw my son. Had he actually followed me to this god-forsaken place to continue his goading? I knew that was silly and figured it to be a shadow of a shrub distorted by moonlight and an agitated imagination. I relaxed and leaned on one of the few standing fence posts.

I saw George Sifkin then.

He frolicked in the moonlight, tossing handfuls of light into the air. No, it wasn't light. It was snow. I could see him laughing but I didn't hear a sound. His jaws were working, grin wide-open and chest heaving.

Suddenly, there were shadows all around me; puncturing the golden glow as they emerged quickly from the darkness surrounding Sifkin's fence.

The townsmen of Shellbank as they had been long ago. The fathers of Potter and Sally and the presider and the Dietz brothers and all the others now haunting the rest home. They had come swiftly and silently from the shadows. And now, they passed over the fence.

They came to George Sifkin, surrounding him and knocking him to the ground. The boy looked around, uncomprehending, his animal innocent eyes probing until they locked onto mine. For an eternal moment, he looked at me beseechingly, his eyes begging, 'what, why'. I averted my eyes and slid back behind the last standing great cedar tree at the corner of the Sifkin place.

They dragged George over the fence, his body going limp as they hauled him into the moonlight. There was no jeering, no cursing or banter of bravado. Just mute, cold concerted rage.

George sobbed uncontrollably, still not understanding. He did nothing to resist. Suddenly, there was another flash of moonlight between branches now swaying in a hot, harsh wind. The tree limbs parted revealing…ME!

My face, its expression uncomprehending and resentful, as I held the other end of a rope to give counterbalance to the weight of George Sifkin's body as it now dangled, lifeless.

It was over quickly. The men cut down and removed George Sifkin's body and dispersed as stealthily as they had come.

It happened the way Sally had described it. I could see her hiding in the reeds, young again yet as old and wrinkled as she was during our interview; frightened yet wide-eyed curious. I saw the Dietz boys, holding their father's horse and Potter pushing back his fishing cap to whistle in amazement like he'd finally hooked the ultimate big one. They were young and old at the same time, ageless and unable ever to be young or old ever again, there and not there. The way I had been.

As the story of Sifkin's fence unfolded yet again on still another hot dark night in Shellbank.

I see them now, the assembled population of Shellbank. I see young Wilfred Dietz, walking up the dirt path leading from the train tracks and the Sifkin place up to the Baptist Church where the crowd had gathered.

I see a distraught man, walking stoically, staring straight ahead of him, stunned. He is carrying the lifeless corpse of his little girl, her smooth white arm dangling. It recalls the scene from the Boris Karloff movie version of the Frankenstein story, after the monster had senselessly killed innocence.

The image is chopped and grainy, interspersed with the vivid color of George Sifkin, playing with his dog, mindless of the madness coming his way from the other side of the fence. Sonorous music underplaying the screams of a father's anguish, then communal rage; all playing in counterpoint to the happy laughter of a boy and barking dog at play.

The sight of the young girl's broken body enrages the townsfolk and they storm the monster's lair; carrying off a witless boy to hang him from the twisted branch of a large cedar tree. His lifeless body left to dangle to appease the crowd's bloodlust as a hot wind blows. A wind that hell released upon Shellbank and hasn't stopped blowing to this day. I see it all again and again as I slump at the foot of the gnarled tree beneath that spot.

Wilfred Dietz found me there the next morning. Unhappy that their breakfasts hadn't been brought out for them, the residents of the home became positively alarmed when no one showed up to dispense morning medications and it was decided to send out a search party to find me.

"I figured I might find you hereabouts." Dietz muttered.

He fidgeted and wouldn't look at me. Reminded me of my son when I'd gone through his gym bag and found a half-dozen hand-rolled cigarettes and I questioned him about it, both of us already knowing that I understood completely what the cigarettes were but me just playing my role. My role with

Dietz, it seemed, was to be that of the browbeater; forcing a reluctant witness who literally knew where the body was buried to come clean. Even though it was apparent by all his fawning and cowering that Dietz really wanted and needed to say it all.

"How is it that your little history neglected to mention what actually happened at Sifkin's fence?" I asked testily.

"Until now, our little community suffered a sort of group amnesia on the subject." Dietz started to assume a pedantic pose, but I responded with the same scowl I'd reserved for my son. Dietz quickly changed his tone.

"Strange things happened there all the time. I was only four years old when the *incident* occurred. No one ever talked about it. I was never sure if it really happened or if it was just a dream or just one of those tricks George was always playing."

Dietz told about the Willard girl who one day decided that she wanted to play with George Sifkin's dog and how she'd climbed over the fence. Instead of the dog, she encountered George who became excited to finally find someone on his side of the fence. George wanted to play. The girl became frightened and tried to run. George became frightened and tried to quiet her by placing his hand over her mouth. But that only frightened the girl more and she struggled. Her struggles confused and frightened George who didn't know what to do. So he held on tighter and tighter.

Until he'd snapped her neck.

A worker coming back from ice house spotted the girl's body lying in the middle of the yard and ran to tell her father…

Dietz told me that, after every one had left the Sifkin place that night, he had stayed, hidden, and watched. When all was quiet, a beam of moonlight suddenly flashed on the hanging tree. And there was George Sifkin, alive again; yanking the rope from the limb and lowering himself to the ground. After he freed himself, he whistled for the dog which came loping out of nowhere.

The two of them then wandered off down the path to the bay, where Henry Sifkin's boats were anchored.

"Last I ever saw of either of them."

The folk of Shellbank had expected Henry Sifkin to exact a terrible revenge. But he didn't. He surprised them all one night by simply leaving Shellbank; taking his family and as many of his possessions as he could carry. Boarding one of his oyster boats, he sailed away into the world.

Shellbank rose the morning after that to find that the boats Henry had left behind had been scuttled beyond repair. The ice house had been burned to the ground as well. Shellbank quickly learned how economically dependent it had been upon the industry of Henry Sifkin.

Soon, the train no longer stopped there because there was no longer any reason to stop. There being no work, the men of Shellbank settled into the vicious hopelessness of the idle. In despair, the people turned to religion and finding no solace there, boarded up the Baptist Church; chasing away the minister. Shellbank died, and began the long process of withering away that produced the dried out husk I discovered years later.

Henry Sifkin had not sought revenge but with his show of noble disdain, he had exacted a terrible retribution from Shellbank by revealing the simple truth about the place and its people.

I had learned from checking the records at the county library and through it, sources elsewhere, that the other children and grandchildren and great-grandchildren of Henry Sifkin had multiplied and spread across America; becoming doctors and lawyers and teachers, statesmen and warriors; people of property and substance; respected members of numerous communities.

While Shellbank dwindled and diminished.

"Didn't the men take the body and bury it in an unmarked grave out in the Great Cedar Swamp?" I asked.

"They did. But I saw what I saw." Dietz replied emphatically. "George and the dog vanished inside a curtain of reeds at the water's edge."

Dietz wearily related how the men of Shellbank began to die off afterward. Some went quickly, from oddball ailments no one had ever heard of; others more slowly, from the effects of alcohol and idleness and guilt.

Some tried to leave, to make new lives for themselves. But they always came back to Shellbank. Alone. Battered bitter by failure. They *had* to come back and live out the lives they had made for themselves in this place.

It would be easy to examine what had happened with the comfortable detachment and wisdom of hindsight afforded by the all-knowing 60's and resolve that George Sifkin had been lynched by an angry white mob because he was black and because he was retarded and because he crossed a line that was not in the least invisible back in "those days".

Dietz explained it better as we sat in the shade of the tree near the remains of Sifkin's fence. He told me that George Sifkin's "difference" didn't really have to do with his skin color or mental state (Although both made it easier in the beginning for the actors to justify what they did during the first of many long lonely conversations each had with himself.).

"He lived in his own world, on the other side of that fence." Dietz said haltingly, still seeking an answer that would be true for himself. "It was a place the rest of us couldn't go. We didn't understand it. It frightened us. It made us angry and we resented him because he was simple and happy. It made him less human and more of an abstract symbol or something, something put here to test and torment the rest of us; something forbidden and out of reach and even though *we* didn't understand, we wanted it. When we couldn't have it, we destroyed it."

I was surprised to see that most of what was left of the community of Shellbank had gathered around us as we talked. There were many sheepish looks, some tearful. All were solemn and anxious. I looked around and nodded, saying nothing. I had nothing to offer them in the way of solace or wisdom. But I was able to suggest that events in histories have beginnings and endings. And it was necessary to end one phase before the next could begin and run its course. I suggested that, perhaps, Shellbank, had not properly concluded the *incident* at Sifkin's fence.

There was no need to submit a written revision of Wilfred Dietz history to the rest home historical club at its next meeting. Without taking any vote or offering any of those "motions" one always hears about at meetings, the group headed en masse over to the long-forgotten Baptist Church. I helped Potter and the presider as they plied away the planks that blocked the front door.

Several of them went inside while the others mingled uneasily at the door. The presider emerged from the church carrying a small wooden cross. Small as it was, it must have weighed heavily because several of the others helped him carry it.

I watched them hobble and limp and shuffle down the dirt path leading back to the Sifkin place. They were hesitant and ashamed, yet they were determined to do what they were doing.

Several others were carrying jars of honey. Sally carried a wreath of dandelions. The presider again took the lead as his father had ages ago as the last minister in the Baptist Church.

After they settled around the last standing fence post, the presider nodded at Wilfred Dietz who propped the cross against the fence post. One by one the others approached bearing the honey and dandelions.

No one looked into the Sifkin yard. Dietz shuffled back to stand beside me under the tree. Sally tried to arrange the flowers but her fingers were trembling so much she made a mess of it. A few of the others shambled forward to help. The presider waited.

It's hot and the oldtimers were wilting quickly. Several lowered themselves awkwardly into the browned grass. Others sought shade under the tree which rattled creaky branches and parched clumps of leaves by way of greeting.

The presider tried some words but he found no comfort in language. Memory ruled here and memory was not showing mercy this day. So the presider let pass the opportunity for ornate oratory.

"We're here to finally recognize a wrong that we, as a community, committed long ago." He said. "We can't go back. And there's not much to look forward to. Perhaps, we do this now that our sin has been finally brought to light, out of fear and selfishness in hopes of assuring ourselves a cleaner slate if and when we meet our maker.

The speech felt wrong. It wasn't about George Sifkin. It was about them. But maybe it was in understanding that it was *they* who needed this, that made the speech right, after all.

"We're sorry George. We didn't know what we were doing." He paused, letting the hot wind off the bay punctuate and carry his speech back to his listeners, through the ages. "Let's go back and try to make some sense with what we have left."

As the presider walked slowly away, he nodded toward the Sifkin house.

A cool breeze, coming from the Sifkin yard, suddenly swept over the place. It ruffled the calico of the dresses and played with the thin strands of hair cobwebbed on the heads of the men. It lifted Potter's fishing cap and sent it dancing ahead of them as they headed back down the path, dust devils clearing the way. I took a long sniff of the air and would have sworn I smelled snow.

"Wonderful." Sally cooed in a girlish voice. "You know, all of a sudden, I feel like going on a picnic." Other voices murmured giddy agreement. Without a word, they shuffled past the rest home and headed toward the marsh. I stood and watched as they vanished, one by one, inside the swaying wall of marsh reeds and phragmites that lined the side of the road.

I did not follow. Instead, I waited by the fence, not knowing why. Did I figure to see George Sifkin, returning at last to complete the pitiful story of this forsaken place? There *was* someone watching me, from the other side of Sifkin's fence.

My son. His shoulder-length hair blowing freely in the breeze, the outlandish outfit, guitar slung over his right shoulder. He smiled and beckoned me with a wave of his hand…

There are places like Shellbank everywhere. We all know of one. We all have a place like it inside ourselves. Places we like to keep locked up, where we're afraid to go because we don't want to discover its secrets and what those secrets tell about ourselves.

But in order to truly live, we must seek those places and know them fully and deal with that knowledge, working with it to allow us to grow and make changes for the better, to make our lives complete.

Now, I know how it should go at the end of a story. Resolution.

I should cross the fence and go to him and let the mystery that still lingers in that place be the guide of my actions. But what mystery? Innocence? Anger? Remorse and reconciliation? I ponder and I actually consider crossing over.

But that would be too easy and I'm not sure that I can give in and throw myself upon another's strength, a magic that isn't really my own, to see me through. So I walk away, choosing instead to follow the double yellow line, leading away from Shellbank.

The direction I take leads along the New Jersey side of Delaware Bay, past places long ago abandoned in man's triumphal march of progress. And eventually to Camden and just beyond that, Philadelphia, and back to familiar places I had fled once in moments of fear and weakness. But even now I was beginning to feel more prepared to properly explore.

978-0-595-36506-7
0-595-36506-X

Printed in the United States
35826LVS00007B/146

9 780595 365067